"Didn't you hear what I said? He's dead. He leaned forward and whispered, "Murdered."

"Murdered?" I mouthed the word. "But how? I mean. . .I talked to him on the phone only yesterday." My response didn't make sense, but I was so shocked I wasn't thinking logically.

"Someone put him away last night." The clerk tugged at his magenta blazer. "I'll probably get in trouble for telling you this, but he was murdered right inside his room. Room 623."

Don't miss out on a single one of our great mysteries. Contact us at the following address for information on our newest releases and club information:

Everybody Wanted Room 623

An "Everybody's Suspect" Mystery

Cecil Murphey

HEARTSONG
PRESENTS
MYSTERIES

For Shirley—who has always been there for me.

ISBN 978-1-59789-711-2

Scripture taken from the HOLY BIBLE, NEW INTERNATIONAL VERSION®. NIV®. Copyright © 1973, 1978, 1984 by International Bible Society. Used by permission of Zondervan. All rights reserved.

All of the characters and events in this book are fictitious. Any resemblance to actual persons, living or dead, or to actual events is purely coincidental.

Cover design: Kirk DouPonce, DogEared Design
Cover illustration: Jody Williams

Our mission is to publish and distribute inspirational products offering exceptional value and biblical encouragement to the masses.

Printed in the U.S.A.

1

When the desk clerk first mentioned Stefan Lauber's death, I didn't react. The truth is, I was only half listening. Although I came to see Stefan, I had agreed to meet him at the Cartledge Inn for my own reason. It was a good excuse to get away from the Clayton County Special Services, where I headed up the mental health unit.

Today I was in an especially low mood. The reason was James Burton. Burton, as he likes everyone to call him, is pastor of a church in this area, and we met at the Georgia coast a few months ago. He's the first genuine Christian with whom I ever talked. That's the trouble. I like him. Okay, more than that, I might even be in love with him, but I don't love his God. That is, I *think* I love Burton—and about four days a week I'm positive that I do. It's been a long time since any man has aroused my emotions like that curly-haired preacher.

Even if I do love him, the friendship can never lead to anything—not even a single kiss. Burton is so stubborn, he wouldn't let anything develop in our relationship—I mean a male-female connection. I can be his parishioner or a professional to whom he refers people in need. (And he's done that twice since we met.)

He also angers me. He's so likable. And kind. Okay, and he's cute—really cute. He's no hunk, but I'd settle for those dark blue eyes, and I'd love to run my fingers through those soft, dark brown curls.

Many times I've wished he'd make some kind of move on me, but he's so hung up on his religious commitment, and I'm too honest to fake the faith.

So that's how all of this started. As I approached the desk of the Cartledge Inn and asked for Mr. Lauber, my thoughts were centered on Burton.

It was the first time I had been to the inn, which was built out of red brick that had weathered and lightened over the decades into a pale, rose-colored patina. The double front door was made of thick, dark cherrywood. The place had originally been an inn, built around 1920, just after World War I. A few years ago, the present owners turned it into a retreat center and motel. It's located about three miles outside of Atlanta's Stone Mountain Park.

Because his words hadn't sunk in, I said to the clerk again, "Lauber. Stefan Lauber."

He stared at me.

"I think he's registered here."

"Didn't you hear what I said? He's dead." He leaned forward and whispered, "Murdered."

"Murdered?" I mouthed the word. "But how? I mean. . .I talked to him on the phone only yesterday." My response didn't make sense, but I was so shocked I wasn't thinking logically.

"Someone put him away last night." The clerk tugged at his magenta blazer. "I'll probably get in trouble for telling you this, but he was murdered right inside his room. Room 623."

The clerk adjusted the pin above his pocket, which read CRAIG BUBECK. "He was a nice man, too, and had been with us for several months. He didn't deserve to get murdered."

I wanted to ask whom he thought deserved to be murdered, but I didn't. Temporarily I had forgotten Burton. Right now I needed to process this information.

"He asked me to come see him this morning," I said, although I was talking to myself more than to the clerk. "He said it was important and. . ." I stopped myself before I began to babble.

"The police were here last night for more than two hours. At least that's what Doris said. She's the other clerk, and sometimes she exaggerates. They came back again this morning. They don't seem to want to stay away. Ghoulish, if you ask me. But after all, how much time do they need to search one room? A hotel room is a hotel room, and I have no idea why they searched the room again and again. I mean, how long does it take to search *one* room?" The fiftyish, wimpish clerk must have tipped the scales at 115 pounds. He rambled on, but I had stopped listening, to his obvious disgust.

"How was he murdered?" I asked to break his monologue.

"Shot. With a gun, you know. Right in the heart. At least that's what I heard." He pulled back slightly and looked around to make sure no one could hear. "I didn't see the body, you understand, but that's what Doris told me this morning. You see, this month, because of vacations, we're doing twelve-hour shifts and—"

"Do they know who did it? Do they know why someone killed Stefan—uh, Mr. Lauber?"

He shook his head. "The police don't know anything, or at least nothing that I've heard. Since you're asking, I'll tell you what I do know. Mr. Lauber called for room service at 4:22 and asked for a meal to be brought to him at 7:00. Wasn't that considerate of him? None of our other guests would think to order in advance. Anyway, when the waiter arrived, he knocked, and no one answered. The door was slightly ajar, so he assumed Mr. Lauber had left it open for him because maybe he was in the shower or something. Just as he pushed the door fully open, he called out, 'Room service.' "

"Yes?" I asked. "And what happened?"

"That's it."

"What do you mean by 'That's it'?"

"The body. Once he had stepped into the room, he spotted Mr. Lauber's body sprawled on the floor, facedown. Blood. Lots of blood."

"That must have been horrible."

"It certainly is. They'll have to replace the carpet. The owners hate it when the inn incurs unexpected expenses like that. He was shot. Didn't I mention that? Shot right in the heart with a .38. I don't know anything about guns, but Doris—"

"The other clerk—"

"Right, Doris told me. I didn't see anything myself, you understand, but this morning one of the detectives stopped at the desk and we talked. He told me a few other facts."

"Really?" I didn't mean anything by the question. I was processing information.

Craig must have assumed I doubted him, so he leaned forward again and whispered, "All right, he didn't actually tell me, but I overheard him on his cell phone when he told someone else. I was clever at it. I kept my back to him so he wouldn't think I was listening, but I heard every word. *Every single word.*"

Stunned, I couldn't say anything, and I must have looked like an utter fool with my mouth hanging open.

"Mr. Lauber didn't suffer, so that's a blessing. I'm sure of that fact, because on his cell, the detective said he died instantly."

I wondered why people thought that the news of instant death was supposed to comfort anyone. Whether they suffered three seconds or ten minutes or died instantly, they were still dead.

"Dead," I said. I finally had enough presence of mind to move away from the front desk. I walked toward two sofas upholstered in apricot-colored fabric. The antique tables matched the walls. The lobby definitely had an elegant look about it. I sat on the end of the sofa and pondered the situation. How odd that Stefan had been insistent—almost demanding—that I come to the inn to see him. He had apologized for asking but said it was extremely important. Now I wondered what "extremely important" meant.

I didn't know Stefan that well. I'm a therapist, and he had started to come to our mental health center. Because I'm the director, I don't see many clients. His coming in itself was odd because he could afford a private therapist. Most of our clients come because they have no insurance and they pay on a sliding scale, which goes all the way down to five dollars a session. Stefan said a friend had recommended me—a psychologist named David Morgan, whom I respected. Stefan freely admitted he could pay, and we billed him at the rate of $60 an hour, which is our highest payment level. The fee hadn't seemed to faze him. Later I realized that money was certainly no problem for him.

At first he came once a week, and then he asked for twice-weekly appointments. "I have a number of things to think through," he said. "Business issues mostly, but being with you pushes me to return to my room and think seriously."

I studied him to be sure he wasn't flirting with me. Not that I would have minded, but I'm a therapist and nothing else, and now and then a man thinks he has to hit on me. I wouldn't have been able to date him if he had asked—which he didn't—but he was still quite a hunk. A little old for me by maybe ten or fifteen years. The wrinkles of wear around his eyes and mouth made him appear to be in his late forties—about ten years older than his actual age—but he could still get any woman's attention when he entered a room.

A week ago he asked if he could see me privately and if I would come to the Cartledge Inn. I don't usually do that, but I sensed he had serious problems—the kind that he was determined to resolve—and I was willing to provide individual attention to such clients. At our center we're moving toward a behavior-model therapy for everything, and we'll eventually do only group counseling to save money. Consequently, we've been mandated to accept fewer individual patients. Even though I granted Stefan personal sessions, he paid the center. I don't do private counseling as a sideline; that had never seemed ethical to me. Because of our policy change, the board of directors encouraged us to take a limited number of private patients if we felt they needed special help.

For the next few months, we're still able to accept patients who can pay the minimum scale or more if we believe they'll benefit. I felt Stefan Lauber was one of those individuals who had made amazing progress and wouldn't need a therapist long.

"Stefan is dead," I said to myself.

I was so caught up in the shock of the news that I didn't notice when someone walked past me to the counter, which was perhaps fifteen feet away. Only when I heard his voice did I look up.

"I'd like a room, please."

"I suppose you want room 623," Craig, the clerk, said.

"Sure, that's fine." His back was to me, but I would have recognized his voice anywhere. Sometimes I hear it in my sleep.

"Everybody wants 623," the clerk said. "And I can't let you have that one."

He chuckled. "Okay, give me something else."

Impulsively I got up and walked toward him. "Burton!"

He turned around and smiled. I hate that smile— it melts me every time. And those dark curls ought to be illegal on a man.

"Julie West!" he called out. "What are you doing here?"

"I came to see someone, but he's not in," I said.

"He's not in because he's dead," the clerk said. "Murdered."

"What's going on?" Burton looked from me to the clerk.

"That's why you can't have room 623," Craig said. "The police won't let me give it to anyone. With blood stains all over the carpet and the room all torn up, I have no idea why anyone would want it anyway."

Burton moved forward and hugged me. It was a nice, friendly, brotherly kind of embrace. "Nice to see you again, Julie."

I hated that I had worn my lime green four-inch heels today. I'm five ten in bare feet and about half an inch taller than Burton anyway. Now I towered above him. But my colors were right. My hair is a shade of red someone called Titian, after the painter, and it sounded exotic to me, so I tell everyone that's my color. *Red* is so, well, mundane. I wore a lime green suit with short sleeves. It wasn't formfitting, but I felt it made the best of my assets. Any shade of green seems to flatter me the most. For jewelry I wore only a copper-and-green malachite bracelet that complemented my complexion and my light brown eyes. I may not have looked chic, but it was my best outfit.

"She wanted to see Mr. Lauber," Craig said. "But then, everyone either wants to see him or wants his room. If you ask me, this is a strange place today."

I stared at the unprofessional clerk. He held a pen in his right hand, but it was shaking. "This has rattled you, hasn't it?" I asked.

"Rattled? That's all I can think about. My nerves are shot. Absolutely shot. I know I won't sleep tonight." He wasn't loud, but his voice had hit the higher registers, signaling that he was near hysteria. "It's bad enough to be a clerk in an inn where someone was murdered, but everyone keeps asking for that room—his room—for room 623. What kind of ghoulish people come here?"

Burton touched the man's hand gently and said, "You have had a bad time of this. I'm sorry." That was Burton in action. I've told him twenty times he ought to be a therapist instead of a pastor, but he has never listened to my advice. Burton's soothing voice worked its magic. "Can you take a few days' vacation or—"

The clerk snorted. "And miss all this action? Nothing like this has ever happened before." He spoke in a normal range again.

"But you are upset," I said. "Don't you think it would help if you took at least a day off?"

"My nerves are shot," he said, "but I'll. . .well, I'll carry on."

Burton continued to speak softly to the clerk, and I nodded at everything he said. That Burton is a natural at getting people to open up to him. Within two minutes the poor man told Burton all his other problems. He said something about his mother, who was in the early stages of senility, and added that he was an only child. He had dated a woman for nine years, and she'd finally called it off. "But as long as I had to take care of Mother, I couldn't have a wife, too, could I?"

I thought it would be more discreet if I moved away, so I went back to the sofa and sat down. I couldn't hear the rest, but within several minutes the man smiled. He grabbed Burton's hand and shook it vigorously.

Burton then came over to the sofa, sat on the other end, and turned toward me. "It's such a surprise to see you."

"A good surprise? Or a shock?" I love to say things like that.

"Good. Always it's good to see you."

"I suppose you want to know why I stopped attending your church."

"Not unless you want to tell me," he said. "But I have missed you. You came five Sundays and attended three of the new believers' meetings."

"You keep score on everyone?"

He grinned, and those perfect, movie-star teeth gleamed. "Sorry. I meant only that I was aware of your not being there. That's all."

"What are you doing here?" I asked. "Okay, I changed the subject, but—"

"I'm here for a private retreat."

"A private retreat? I don't get it. It sounds like something a priest or a monk would do." As I said, I love being a smart-mouth. I knew differently, but it also kept him talking to me.

"It's something I do at least once a year. Ben and Marcia Cartledge, the couple who own this place, are wonderful Christians, and they're members of an inner-city congregation. They offer free facilities for ministers of any denomination who need to spend a few days alone."

"Oh," I said. That's always an appropriate response when I don't know what to say.

"Occasionally I need to put my life on hold while I rethink my priorities," he said simply. "It's nice—really it is—to see you again."

"You've already said that. So it means we must be near the end of things to talk about."

"Or maybe we just need to get beyond the awkward stage," he said. "I'm absolutely surprised to run into you here."

"Remember when we met?" I asked. "That involved a murder, too—Roger Harden."

He aimed that powerful smile at me before he said, "You know, I just thought of the same thing."

Burton and I had been involved in solving the murder of Roger Harden at Palm Island off the coast. It was because of our meeting that I started to attend his church. I never told him, of course, but I was more fascinated by him than any of the things he said. He was probably a fine preacher. That hadn't been the reason I attended.

Just then an attractive woman in her early thirties brushed past us and stopped at the desk. "I'd like a room," she said. "I'd like room 623, please."

Craig glanced at us, shrugged, and rolled his eyes as if to ask, *"See what I mean?"*

2

I'm sorry, ma'am," the desk clerk said to the woman in a controlled voice but loud enough for us to hear. "Room 623 is not available."

"Oh, that's too bad. I spent my honeymoon here," she said. "I love that room. Are you sure it's not available?"

"Positive, but I can give you an excellent room on another floor."

Whatever Burton had said to the poor clerk had changed him into a quiet, controlled professional.

"Perhaps the room next to it, then," she said.

"I am sorry, ma'am, but the rooms on either side, 621 and 625, are also taken."

"Are you sure?"

"Yes, ma'am, but I'll check anyway." He paused, clicked a few keys, and stared at the screen. "Yes, ma'am. They are both occupied, and—"

"Across the hall, then?"

"I was about to tell you that rooms 622, 624, and 626 are also occupied. Though two of those will be vacant later today. However, I can give you a lovely room on the floor above. Room 723 is vacant and has the same dusty salmon color with a soft turquoise base as 623. Both rooms offer a superb view of the lake, which is the reason most guests want a room on the north side. In fact, some of our guests have thought rooms 723 and 823 have an even better view because—"

"No, no, that won't do," she said. She stood there,

apparently in contemplation. Her back was to me, but her burnt orange acrylic nails tapped the counter. "I so wanted to stay there. You see, my husband died three months ago. Our plan had been to come here for our tenth anniversary. That's tomorrow."

She was a tall, beautifully built woman. Because I couldn't see her face, I shifted my position. I still couldn't see, so I held up my hand for Burton to wait, and I walked within five feet of her and behind the desk as if I were going down one of the two passageways. I stopped and examined her closely for a few seconds. That's just the way I am: I'm curious about people, especially one as unusual as this woman.

My presence didn't matter; she seemed lost in her own thoughts and unaware that I had approached the desk. She wore a simple navy blue tailored suit that showed her figure to full advantage. Her cloth-covered pumps were obviously made to match the suit. She had curly black hair that barely brushed her shoulders. I figured the hair was probably dyed because the color was too perfect. She had high cheekbones and the classical line of nose and chin. Her skin texture was smooth. She would have been a beautiful woman except that only her mouth smiled. Her dark eyes remained expressionless. I thought that full, rich mouth had probably become quite accomplished at showing the full range of human emotion, but the eyes looked as if they were dead. If eyes are the windows to the soul, no one could see inside that woman.

Her thick, dark hair fell across one eye, and she pushed it away from her face. That drew my attention and I stared at those acrylic nails. Why would anyone choose such an outlandish color? Except for those nails, she could have been a model—an older version—but she definitely had that kind of beauty.

I might have remained focused on the nails except that I knew she had lied to the clerk. I could tell by her body posture. Most people have some giveaway signals, and the way she held her body was my clue. I wondered why she concocted such a story. Who cared why she wanted the room?

I walked back and sat down next to Burton. He knew me well enough that he didn't say anything. He, too, watched the action at the desk.

"I do apologize, ma'am," the clerk said to her, "but it's not—"

"Surely there is some way. If you would explain my situation to the person who currently occupies room 623—"

"I'm sorry. It truly is not available."

"But please. Maybe I could talk to him, or her, or whoever." Her right hand held up two twenty-dollar bills.

The clerk's eyes focused on the money before he said, "I'm sorry."

She added two more bills.

Even I could see the temptation in Craig's eyes, and before she could interrupt him again, he said, "You see, the police have, uh, sealed off that room. There was a crime committed there. You know, like on television—"

"That's terrible. How soon will they finish?" Her hand dropped to the counter, and I couldn't see what she did with the bills.

This time he shrugged. "I can give you 423 or 523. Would that work for you?"

"When will the room be available?" The voice was louder and slightly harsh.

"I don't know. Maybe not for days," he said. "The police wouldn't tell me."

She mumbled something and turned away. She stuffed something inside her shoulder bag, and I assumed it was the money that Craig had reluctantly turned down.

I marveled at her again. I revised my opinion: She wore a little too much makeup, but it was expertly applied. Everything about her was perfect, everything except for those garish nails.

At that moment she turned my way and our eyes met. She must have realized I had been listening, because she smiled with only her mouth while those lifeless eyes stared at me. She cleared her throat, and I sensed she wanted me to think she was slightly embarrassed. "Just seems terrible for a murder to take place in such a quiet setting."

"How did you know it was a murder?" I asked.

"Oh, uh, I assumed. . ."

Again I knew she was lying, and I wondered why. So what if she knew it had been a murder? What was the big deal?

She turned again and faced the clerk. "All right, give me a room as close to 623 as you can, on the north side of the building."

"As you like." He attempted a professional smile. He wasn't gifted that way, and his smile appeared forced. He would have done better to have remained expressionless.

He clicked on his keyboard, but I believe he already knew what rooms were available. "I can give you 629 or 631 or—"

"Fine. Anything. Give me 629."

He handed her a form to fill out and asked for her credit card. I don't know why I watched, but I did. For a second time, I got up from the sofa and edged closer so I could hear and observe everything.

"Thank you, Ms. Knight." He laid the credit card imprint on the counter for her to sign before handing her a key. "We still use keys here instead of the magnetically keyed cards. Our owners think it retains more of the ambiance of a quaint and quiet—"

"Whatever," she said, grabbing the key and walking toward where I assumed the elevators were. Because she didn't hesitate, it was obvious she really had been here before. Maybe she had come on her honeymoon. But after ten years, would she still remember which way to the elevators? Maybe she wouldn't.

As soon as she was out of view, Burton turned to me. "Doesn't that strike you as odd? Several people wanting room 623?" He got up and walked to the desk. "How many people have asked for 623?"

"Three. Maybe four. Five. I don't remember, but this is strange," the clerk said. "I mean really strange, as in insane. The police haven't released the information that he was murdered in room 623, only that a man was found dead in the Stone Mountain area. They certainly didn't say it happened here at the Cartledge Inn, and I've watched the news on CNN and Channel 2. So why would all these people want the same room?"

"Yes, that is strange," Burton said.

"Bizarre," Craig said.

Again Burton asked for a room and told Craig he had a reservation. He added, "You can put me anywhere you want." He pulled a card from his wallet. "This is to show I'm an ordained minister and—"

The clerk nodded. "Thank you." He found the reservation and said, "Yes, there is no charge for the room." He asked Burton how long he planned to stay (three nights) and gave him room 430. "Unless you don't want to be part of this ongoing stream of traffic; in that case I can put you in 315 or 316—that's in the south wing."

"That's fine. I don't need traffic." He smiled and added, "I came here to be alone."

After Burton filled out the information card and received his key, he turned to me. "It's been good to see you again," he said. "My luggage is in the car, so I suppose I'd better get it." He started to walk toward the entrance.

I didn't want him to walk away, but I couldn't think of anything to hold him. As I turned around, I bumped into a tall, broad-shouldered man.

"Sorry, miss," he said.

"Ollie! What are you doing here?" Burton called out. He turned around and walked back over to the man. They did the male, A-frame-hug thing with about five pats on each other's back, which doesn't make any sense to me.

"Hey, Julie," Burton said, "I want you to meet an old friend of mine." He introduced him as Oliver Viktor. They had been classmates in college. "Ollie was a member of our church for a couple of years until he moved over here to the east side of town. What was that? Five years ago?"

"Yeah, five or six."

I smiled at Ollie, but I immediately didn't like him, and I wasn't sure why. I usually like most people, so I figured my reaction spoke more about me than it did about Ollie.

"This is the man who tried to lead me astray many times!" Burton said and laid his arm on his friend's shoulder. "We did a lot of crazy things in college—"

"No, *you* did the crazy things," Ollie said. "I was merely the mastermind behind the brilliant ploys and fabulous activities."

Burton laughed. "He's right, you know. He was the trickster—"

"The brilliant thinker and mastermind genius is what this low-level pastor means—"

"Uh, as I said, Ollie was the trickster and planner behind a lot of pranks and—"

"But always in good taste," Ollie said.

"Oh, really?" Burton looked at me. "Good taste? How does this sound? We had a boring speaker at our commencement—"

"Boring sounds mild," Ollie said, but he grinned and obviously enjoyed this trip down memory lane. "I felt I was doing something uncommonly good for the entire graduating class."

"We'd heard that speaker a couple of times before—"

"And he always ran over the allotted time when he spoke." Ollie shook his head and frowned. "That's what got me the most. If they allotted him thirty minutes, he took forty or forty-five—"

"Right, so Ollie got the idea of how he could shut him up." Burton blushed and looked away to hide it. "What we did. . .well, it—it wasn't kind."

Ollie shrugged. He looked like a man who shrugged a lot. "We weren't trying to be kind. Only effective. And it was fun."

"Okay, yes, to a couple of twenty-two-year olds, it *seemed* like fun when we planned it, but—"

"It was fun," Ollie said, "and it worked."

I had already entered Zone Total Boredom by then and I honestly didn't care, but it was obvious that such pranks were an important part of their relationship. So I asked the right question: "What outrageous things did you two guys do at your commencement?"

Burton rewarded me with one of his heart-melting smiles. "Uh, well—"

"The president of the college knew I was into all kinds of—uh, well, youthful pranks," Ollie interrupted in a voice he intended to come across as modest. "So I had to divert him."

"Yeah, divert is right." Burton shook his head, and his eyes made me realize he thought it was a terrible thing to do. "You see, Julie, it did seem like fun at the time. We thought only of ourselves, not about the feelings of anyone else or—"

"Hey, don't start that," Ollie said. "He was a stuffy jerk, and he deserved what happened. So tell her."

"Ollie convinced me to give up my alarm clock and set the alarm for 4:00—the time the speaker, Dr. Garrar Terashita, was scheduled to end."

"What a hoot! What pandemonium!" Ollie laughed

and whacked Burton on the shoulder. "The old buzzard was in the middle of a sentence, and the alarm rocked the building. Everyone just stared for a minute or so. They couldn't figure out what caused the noise or where it came from. Seven of us knew what was going on, and we laughed the loudest—"

"I didn't laugh," Burton said. "I saw that poor man's face and realized what a mean—"

"Oh yeah, I forgot," Ollie said. "And after the ceremony, my good friend lectured me over the evils of our ways. That's what he said, but I really think he was most upset because he had lost his alarm clock." Ollie winked at me as if I were supposed to laugh with him.

I didn't laugh.

"Yes, it was insane with noise. Our little group laughed," Burton said, "but I felt sorry for the faculty, especially the president and the others sitting behind Dr. Terashita."

"What happened?" I asked. "I assume they figured out the source of the noise." I didn't like playing the straight role for Burton's comic friend, but I felt I had to do it.

"Finally the dean of students and a couple of the profs ran toward the podium." Ollie's voice had become louder, and he roared as if it were the first time he had ever told of his great escapade. "It took the dean a few more seconds to find the alarm clock. You know why? Because I had taken Burton's clock and buried it inside the flower stand that was in front of that podium."

That still didn't seem funny to me, but I hadn't been there, so maybe it had been funny. Regardless, in my newly volunteered role, I knew the next question to ask. "Did you get into trouble?"

"Nah," Ollie said. "They questioned me, and I said, 'I did not put that alarm clock inside the flower stand'—deep inside so they had to remove the flowers to get to it." He winked at me. "See, I told the truth."

"That was because they didn't ask if you had planned it."

Ollie shrugged. "But Burton here was such a good boy, no one ever would have suspected he would do such a devious thing."

"So you got away with it?"

"We got away with it, but—"

"But what?" I asked. There. I had done my duty. That would be my last question.

"Preacher boy confessed."

"You did *what*?" I hadn't planned to ask that one, but it made me respect Burton a lot more. Not that I needed to respect him more. "That must have taken a lot of guts."

"I don't know about guts," Burton said. "What we did wasn't right, and it disrupted everything. Dr. Terashita was so embarrassed and hurt that he didn't try to finish his speech. As he threw his papers together, I saw the pain in his eyes, and I knew I had done a rotten thing." He turned his gaze toward Ollie. "And it was a very, very mean thing to do."

"Aw, c'mon, it was fun—"

"Not that one." Burton shook his head. "But the other things this evil genius did weren't so bad. At least that's the only time I was aware of someone being hurt."

"What about the effigy?" Ollie prompted. As he said

those words, I began to realize why I didn't like him.

"I didn't have anything to do with that, and if I had known, I would have refused to participate," Burton said. "It was one of your few plans I refused to join in with. Remember?"

"Yeah, I forgot. You had gotten so lame by then, but that was all right, because I got some other guys—guys who appreciated a good joke."

I hoped we were ready to move on, but Ollie explained that he detested one professor, the man who taught most of the required English classes. "Boring old guy," Ollie muttered. So he talked two other students into helping him. They stole a scarecrow from a farmer's field, hung it in the quadrant, wrote the professor's name on a placard, and pinned it to its chest. "You know, I can't remember the old buzzard's name."

"Hawkins. Dr. Robert Hawkins IV," Burton said softly. "I liked him and learned from him—"

"Oh yeah, maybe you did, but he bored me."

"Are you easily bored?" I asked and hoped that would change the subject.

Ollie shrugged for the third time. I had been correct—he was one of those frequent shruggers. But then, he had the shoulders for it. "Oh, before you ask, I'll bet you can't guess why I'm here."

"It certainly can't be to ask for room 623, can it?" That was a smart-mouthed remark said in my most sarcastic tone. I felt I was back in my own territory—at last.

"How did you know about that room?" Ollie stared at me and seemed genuinely surprised.

This time I shrugged—exaggerating the movement

for his benefit. I don't think he caught my mockery.

"Hey, I don't know how you figured that out," Ollie said, "but yeah, that's why I'm here. It's room 623. But how—"

"The clerk told us," Burton said quickly. He knows me, and he could see I was getting ready to make another smart remark.

"Okay, okay, dumb clerk," Ollie said. He turned to me and grinned. I think he thought his conversation charmed me. Okay, for some women that would have been charming, especially when those green eyes lit up. I admitted to myself that he was as handsome as any man I'd ever met. He probably pumped iron five hours every day. His ash blond hair had barely begun to recede on top, so it was nice to see that he was flawed, even if only a little.

"You see, Julie, I work for the DeKalb County Police Department. I'm here to investigate a murder."

"A murder?" I said and batted my eyes a couple of times. I figured out that the Cartledge Inn was in DeKalb County and not inside Stone Mountain, which made it a county matter.

"Yeah, scary stuff, huh?"

"The murder? Who was murdered?" Burton asked.

"Stefan Lauber," I said. "In room 623. Right, Detective?"

"Yeah, that's right."

"Who was he?" Burton asked.

Ollie held up his hand. "Wait a minute, missy. How do you know about this murder and his name? Don't tell me the clerk blabbed that much. We haven't released his name to the public."

"Not exactly the clerk's fault," I said because I didn't want to cause any trouble for Craig. "I'm a therapist. Stefan is a client. . .was a client, and—"

"And you make house calls?" There was that grin again, but it soon disappeared as the upper lip curled into a sneer.

I wanted to slap the expression off his face, but I restrained myself. "Not ordinarily, but this was special," I said. "Mr. Lauber asked me to come here. He said it was extremely important."

Ollie's eyes traveled from my head to my feet and back to my face. "Yeah, I can guess that it was special."

His attitude shocked me so badly I was momentarily speechless. If I had been fifteen years old, I would have punched him in the nose, regardless of his size.

"She really is a therapist," Burton said.

"Okay, so you're a real shrink," he said. "Sorry if I misunderstood, but with looks like yours and—"

"Let's leave it at that," I said.

He gave another shrug. "Lauber told you it was extremely important, or so you said?"

"That's correct. *He* said it was extremely important."

"In what way?" Ollie asked. "What made it important? Was it also urgent?"

I smiled softly to deflect my response. "As I've already said, I'm his therapist. That's privileged and confidential information." I knew I could tell him what he wanted to know, but I've heard that line in so many movies, I wanted to use it. It felt good to say those words.

"But he's dead now. So you can tell me, right?"

"It was confidential. He bared his soul to me

because he trusted me."

"What do I care about his bared soul? You want to help us catch the murderer," Ollie said, "so come on, open up."

I didn't want to tell him anything except to say firmly, "Get out of here and leave us so I can talk to Burton." But there was something else. I couldn't understand why I hesitated. Ollie was a detective, and I couldn't think of a single reason not to tell him everything, but that intuitive nudge held me back.

Something about that detective bothered me, and I no longer blamed it on myself. This man's hat wasn't worn right, as my dad used to say. I stared at his ash blond hair, his green eyes. I estimated him at about six three or perhaps even an inch taller. Broad-shouldered, he had probably played football in college. I suppose it was his attitude that put me off. Maybe he was used to pushing people around. When he talked, it was almost as if he expected people to give him whatever he wanted—as if it were his right. Maybe that's why Burton had yielded to him in college. Ollie must have always been heavy-handed and demanding like that.

"I thought you detectives always came in pairs," I said in what I hoped was my innocent voice. "You know, so that one keeps the other honest."

"Yeah, usually. Two police officers investigated last night—"

"And you can handle everything by yourself?" (I knew he wouldn't catch the sarcasm.)

"Yeah, sure, but that's not the reason. In follow-up work like this, they usually send only one detective."

"I'm sure you'll do a thorough job," Burton said.

"Could we get out of here?" I asked as a ploy so I could do some quick thinking. "This is rather public, and you're asking about a man's inner life." Instead of waiting for him to take charge, I started to walk toward the front door and smiled to myself. It felt good to take control of the situation, even if it would last only another twenty seconds.

I turned and he followed. I motioned for Burton to join us, and to my delight he raised his right eyebrow as if to ask, "Me?" I nodded and said, "Sure. Come and join us." I turned forward and moved on. I heard Burton's footsteps behind me. From the front door, I spotted a sign with arrows that read NATURE WALK. Apparently I could have turned either way. I read once that most people automatically turn right, so I turned left.

Although I had never been to the Cartledge Inn before, people who live in metro Atlanta know the grounds are lovely, featuring large sections of native Georgia plants. According to a small sign at the far end, we could walk among forty buddleia bushes of five different colors. Buddleia was one of the few names I knew, although most people just call them butterfly bushes. I love the fragrance the plant sends out and the constant attraction of butterflies and bumblebees.

Because I wore my heels, I used that as an excuse to walk slower. I didn't know how much to tell Burton's buddy, and the walk gave me almost a full minute to think. A slight breeze caused the rosemary plants' evergreen needle–like leaves to hang heavily in the air.

About thirty feet ahead, I saw two comfortable-looking benches that faced each other. They had been placed between Southern magnolia trees. It was early

June, and several of their creamy white flowers already filled the branches. I think the magnolia is not only the most fragrantly beautiful tree, but the flower itself has such a fragile look. I have rarely seen anything nicer than the white blossoms, although I hate the long, hard leaves that take four or five years to become mulch. Still, the flowers are worth the nuisance of the leaves.

I sat on one bench. Ollie and Burton took the other. I knew Burton well enough to know that he wanted to be alone for his private retreat, but he was also curious enough that he didn't want to leave and miss out on the conversation. I smiled to myself, because I was quite sure I was reading his struggle accurately.

Somewhere behind me the overpowering fragrance of honeysuckle wafted through the air. I don't mind honeysuckle, but it causes some people to sneeze or develop sinus headaches. I didn't like it today because the cloying fragrance overwhelmed the magnolia.

"So what can you tell me?" Ollie asked, leaning toward me.

"Aren't you supposed to take out a pen and a little notebook?" I asked. "They always do that on *Law and Order*."

"This is just plain law. Georgia law and my order," Ollie said, impatience apparent in his voice.

"That's a good line," I said. "Do you use it often?"

"Nah. Just popped out." He smiled, oblivious to my sarcasm.

Most women would have called him a hunk, and I suppose he was. Underneath the gray shell blazer, I sensed he had taut, well-toned muscles.

"What do you want to know?" I decided not to

make it easy for him.

Burton leaned forward. "Julie, please don't. Be nice to the man. Okay?"

"You know me too well," I said to Burton. "Okay, here it goes. First, did you know Stefan Lauber had been in prison?"

"Tell me about that," Ollie said. He took out the obligatory notebook and pen. This time he played the role of a cool cop. He wanted information, but he wasn't going to tell me anything he knew.

"Suppose you tell me about his prison term, and then I'll tell you why he came to see me." I stared into his eyes, daring him to intimidate me.

"How well do you know this dame?" he asked Burton.

"Dame?" I said and laughed. "That sounds like something Humphrey Bogart would have said in a 1941 movie. In fact he did say that in the *Maltese Falcon*, didn't he?"

"We just bumped into each other a few minutes ago," Burton said, "but Julie and I were involved in solving the murder of Roger Harden, the multimillionaire. Do you know about that case?"

"Yeah, that's right. I saw it reported on TV, but I had forgotten. Great amateur work, but this is a professional investigation and—"

"Very good," I said. "And since we're all professionals, let's share." This time I not only told him I was a therapist but added that I held a PhD (and that did impress him). "And Burton—"

"Yeah, he's got a doctorate as well. I'm lucky to have finished college and received an undergrad degree. So we're all professionals, but different kinds of professionals." He stared back as if daring me to argue.

"You share. I share," I said. "If you don't want to share, you'll have to get a legal order for me to talk to you." I didn't know if that was true, but the police shows use that kind of insipid dialogue, and it felt good to repeat the words.

"Hey, Burton. It's easy to see why you like this broad. She's a real hottie and she's—"

"A broad? A hottie?" I stood up. "Obviously, this is not a meeting of *professionals*." I wasn't really offended. I liked the crude flattery, but I wouldn't let him know that.

"Ma'am, I apologize," he said with exaggerated emphasis. He spoke the words, but his eyes told me his apology was insincere.

"So you start." I gave him what I call my alluring smile, the kind that's supposed to make others think I'm enchanted with everything that pours from their lips. "You already knew he was in prison, right?" I decided to throw that in so he could see that I used my professional intuition. Actually it was only a guess, but his face told me I was correct.

"Very good. I'm impressed." Ollie rewarded me with a full grin. "Yes, I knew he was in prison. He received a three-year sentence for receiving stolen goods. Which was all they could convict him of. That is, they found the stolen money but not the diamonds—"

"I think I remember that case," Burton said. "It was a jewel robbery of a courier from Antwerp."

"Amsterdam," Ollie corrected. "The courier carried about one hundred million dollars worth of polished diamonds and half a mil in cash."

Ollie told us the background. A known criminal, Willie Petersen, and a woman later identified as Cynthia Salzmann ambushed the man in the long-term parking lot of Hartsfield-Jackson Airport. Apparently the man struggled, and in the altercation, Petersen shot him. The couple fled with the pouch of diamonds and money. Forensics was able to lift Petersen's fingerprints from the door of the courier's car, and the police tracked him down. When accused, he implicated Lauber.

"I wasn't involved in that case," Ollie said, "but I've read the report. They found the cash, which Lauber said Petersen had brought to him and asked him to invest. According to Lauber, who was a legitimate investment broker, Petersen said he had never trusted banks and had been saving the money in his home, or some incredibly dumb story like that."

"But Petersen said Lauber had planned the heist. Wasn't that the story?" Burton asked.

"Exactly. Lauber was a stockbroker. In the previous few months, the SEC and the police suspected—" He held up his hand and said, "Only *suspected*, but were unable to prove, that he was involved in several shady dealings. When it finally came to trial, it was his word against Petersen's."

"That hardly seems like enough to convict anyone," I said.

"Petersen had brought the money into Lauber's office in cash. All in hundred-dollar bills, all still banded with the name of an Amsterdam bank. The information was in the media. Now how many people would have blithely accepted that much cash without some questions?"

"Good point," I said.

"So the jury convicted him. If Lauber had reported the money, nothing would have happened. But the dumb jerk stuck the money in an office closet, and get this—" Ollie raised his voice as he added, "Not only was the money there intact, but it was still in the attaché case that Petersen had stolen. The name of the diamond-polishing firm was on the case—Coster— one of the best-known firms in Europe. The name was right on the case. Petersen insisted Lauber was the brains behind the robbery."

"Didn't they connect Lauber with the diamonds?" I asked.

"They tried, but they had no case," the detective said. "They didn't find the diamonds in his office or anyplace else they searched."

"A jury did convict Lauber, but only of receiving stolen property, is what I remember," Burton said.

"And what about the diamonds?" I asked. "What happened to them?"

"They never turned up. Dead end no matter where the investigation went. I've always believed Lauber hid them and had them ready for a nice retirement plan when he was paroled about five months ago."

"So you think Lauber was murdered for the diamonds?" I asked.

"Reasonable guess, wouldn't you say?" Ollie said. "But we have absolutely nothing to link him to the diamonds. The missing diamonds aren't within my purview—"

"Purview? Nice word," I said.

Burton frowned at me.

"Makes good sense," I said.

"I wish I knew a little more about Stefan Lauber," Ollie said and leaned back. "Now why don't you talk to me? So far I'm the only one giving information. Now it's your turn, so you can help me learn something more about Lauber."

"I also can speak to the answer of that question," a man's voice said. "Did I not know him? Was I not his friend?"

All of us looked up and stared at a man with the smoothest ebony complexion I'd ever seen.

3

Yes, for a long time I have known Mr. Stefan Lauber," the man said as he walked from behind one of the magnolia trees. I hadn't seen him approach, and his presence took us by surprise. I wondered if he had been hiding behind one of the trees.

Not only his syntax but his accent made it clear that he was an African. All the black men I had ever seen were one shade of brown or another, but this man was truly black. His head was shaved, although he had roots for a full head of hair. I assumed he was in his early thirties or maybe late twenties. He was about my height, when I don't wear my heels. He looked healthy enough, but he also was like a man whose skin was stretched over a live skeleton. I didn't know how he could be so thin and yet not look emaciated. Maybe it was his grin and the beautiful white teeth that made me know he was strong, wiry, and healthy.

"And who are you?" Ollie asked.

"Was I not listening to what you say here?"

"I suppose you were," I said. "And you knew Stefan Lauber. How? What was your connection?"

"May I sit with you?" he asked. Without waiting for a reply, he came around and sat on the bench next to me. He wore a plain white T-shirt and sharply pressed shorts, bright red and made of coarse cotton, like muslin.

"My name is Jason Omore," he said, "and I am from Kenya, and I am the grandson and the son of a chief of the Luo tribe from Suna Location." He held out both hands to me and asked my name. After I told him, he turned to Burton and then to Ollie.

"What do you have to tell us?" Ollie asked instead of giving his name.

"Please indulge my cultural background," Jason said. "In my country it is not polite to discuss anything if we are not introduced."

Ollie must have realized the sensible thing to do was to introduce himself, so as to not antagonize the man. He gave his name and said he was a DeKalb County homicide detective. "And now, tell us something besides your name."

"I am here to study as a foreign student, and I am enrolled at Emory University where I am writing my dissertation."

"A dissertation? That means a doctoral degree." I looked at Jason, but I said that for Ollie's benefit. I'm sure he knew, but I wanted to antagonize him a little more.

"In what field?" Burton said a little too quickly. He must have sensed my attitude and tried to intervene.

"In the field of behavioral psychology. Has not my government sent me here to earn my doctoral degree so that I may return and teach behavioral psychology?" He smiled, and his face seemed to glow. "I did my intern work at the Floyd County Prison in Rome." He meant Rome, Georgia, which is about an hour north of us under good driving conditions. "Mr. Lauber was an inmate, was he not? I was able to have many interviews with him. As a matter of great fact, I did a case study of six different inmates. He was the most fascinating, was he not?"

"Do you always give information by asking a question?" Ollie asked.

"Do I?" He laughed. "It is a habit. You Americans seem to like that style, so I have cultivated it. And now I use it often, do I not?"

Burton burst out laughing, and so did I.

"I don't like it," Ollie said.

"Should I then choose not to use it?"

"That's enough," Ollie said. He had obviously figured out that he had become the butt of the joke. "Tell me what you know about Lauber."

Jason Omore was sharp. He was my kind of man.

"He was a criminal and convicted of a lesser crime for which he had committed a greater crime," the African said. "He is—he was—a most complex man and one that many thought had no conscience. Even I did not think so during the first two interviews I had with him."

"But you changed your mind about him?" I asked before Ollie could stop me.

"Yes, that is so. I changed my mind because he changed his way."

"He changed? He reformed? Is that what you mean?" Burton asked. "Or did he just hold back at first?"

"Is that not a good question you have asked about Lauber?" Jason gazed into space as if to measure his words. "I shall have to consider that."

Jason's gaze shifted among our faces. In the distance someone started a lawn mower. The constant rustle of leaves and the gentle breeze against my bare arms felt good. I love Atlanta weather, although the humidity is sometimes a little much for tourists. A male and female cardinal flew into the closer magnolia tree and flitted around for several seconds. I assumed it was some kind of mating dance.

As we waited for Jason to continue, Ollie tapped his foot. His eyes hardened. His chin jutted out. He had all the signs of a man of intense anger. I wondered if he'd explode at me. Maybe I could help him a little and see how long it took.

"I shall tell you, but sometimes you Americans do not seem to understand." He took a deep breath. "Mr. Lauber underwent a conversion experience less than two weeks before his release."

"A conversion? You mean like being born again?" Burton asked.

"Yes, is that not so? Is that not exactly what I mean?" Jason smiled at him. "So you do know the meaning of such language?"

"I'm a pastor. I've also undergone a conversion experience, have I not?"

I couldn't help myself. I roared at Burton's response because I knew he felt as I did about Jason.

Ollie only tapped his foot faster.

"Ah, then you do understand. That is most good."

"Just get on with it," Ollie said. "We're all Christians, okay? We understand the lingo."

I didn't know whether to object to the label that included me, but it didn't seem appropriate to correct Ollie, so I kept still. Besides, I wanted to hear the story.

Jason told us that Lauber made drastic changes in his behavior. "Because you understand the language,

I can say it to you in the language of Christians, may I not?" Before Ollie could interrupt, he said, "My friend—that is, Mr. Lauber, who became my friend—truly repented of his sinful ways and chose to follow the Lord Jesus Christ and was baptized while he was an inmate in prison. Is that not the way it is done here in America, as well?"

"Yes, that's the way," Burton said. He laid a hand on Ollie's shoulder. It was obvious Burton had realized Jason wasn't going to go any faster or give any more information than he chose. It was also obvious that Ollie's irritation was nearing the explosion point.

"That is also why I am here at the Cartledge Inn to work. Mr. Lauber became not only my friend, but my mentor, as well. He has paid for me to stay here in this place for six months. I could have stayed near Emory and worked part-time, but he chose to help me. I think it will not take me much longer to finish my dissertation and then to defend it. Is that not so?"

"Probably," I said and intentionally veered from the subject of Stefan Lauber. "It took me about five months, and I did nothing else. I was exhausted when I finished mine."

"Can we get back on topic?" Ollie asked. It was obvious that he was working hard to control his voice.

"Yes, and there is one thing more I can tell you," Jason said. "Because you are an *askari*—pardon, I mean a policeman, I think this is what you must want to know. Mr. Lauber had in his possession a certain number of stolen diamonds." He paused and stared at the detective. "You knew that much, did you not?"

4

Y ou *knew* Stefan had the diamonds?" I asked Jason. "So he was involved in the theft."

He nodded. "And does not this policeman also know that fact?"

As we sat outside the Cartledge Inn, Jason Omore's words shocked us. Or maybe they shocked only me. Ollie jumped from the bench and took a step forward, almost as if he were intent on grabbing Jason's T-shirt, but Burton's arm on his shoulder pulled him back.

"Easy, my friend," Burton said softly.

"But you know—you know for certain that he was in possession of the diamonds?" Ollie's voice grew louder.

"If your question is to ask if I saw the diamonds, the answer, of course, is that I did not see them."

"So you don't know—"

"But if you want to know what he told me—told me but did not show me—then, yes, I can tell you most assuredly that Mr. Lauber had the diamonds."

I liked Jason better all the time. He had that delightful sense of humor I love in people. He might be a foreigner, but he knew how to get to people like Ollie.

"Of course that's what I want to know." Ollie sighed loudly. "Are you trying to play some kind of game with me?"

"Would I do such a thing?" Jason asked.

Ollie glared at him.

"But, yes, to respond to your question, Stefan had possession of the diamonds. He also told me that he planned to return them. Did you not know that as well?"

"How would I know?" Ollie said.

"Is that not why you have come?"

"I came to investigate his *death*," Ollie said, and it was obvious from the tight-lipped way he spoke that he was nearing the explosion point. "A few people in law enforcement assumed Lauber had the stones, but we could never prove it. If we could have proven it, he would still be in prison."

"Did you believe he had them?" I asked.

"I came to finish up the report on the death of a man in this hotel. Just that."

"Did you know he had the stolen diamonds?" Burton asked me. "I mean, when he met with you, did he admit that to you?"

"He never said anything directly to me about them." I thought about my last conversation with Stefan. "I wonder if that's why he wanted me to meet him here. . .to talk about them."

"Yes, is that not so?" Jason said. "He told me that he was going to speak with you today because you are a person of good conscience."

"Good conscience?" I laughed. "What does that mean?"

"Those were his true words. He also told me that he would compensate you well for your efforts. More than that, I cannot say. My *rafiki*—my friend—told me he trusted you. That is how much I know."

"That's news to me," I said, but I felt quite flattered.

"Yes, it may be news to you," Jason said, "but I know he trusted you and wanted you to be the one to return the diamonds."

"Me? Why would he ask me to—"

"So where are the diamonds?" Ollie interrupted. "You said you haven't seen them, but do you know where they are?"

Jason shook his head. "No, it is true that I have not seen them, *bwana*—uh, sir. He said he had placed them in a safe place. 'A very safe place' were his exact words. He said he placed them there before he went into *gaol*—uh, prison. He told me that he also had funds—large sums of money—secreted in a total of twelve places, but I do not know where, so do not, please, to ask that question."

"I'm trying to get all the information I can," Ollie said. He scribbled a few notes in his notebook. "And I think you have more to tell me, so how about if—" Ollie's cell phone buzzed, and he excused himself and walked about ten feet away. He turned his back to us. We could hear nothing—and it wasn't that I didn't try to listen.

As he stood there, I detected a slight tremor in his right hand. *Nerves?* I wondered.

He closed his phone, turned toward us, and said, "I have to leave now." His gaze shifted to the African. "I know where to reach you, Jason, so don't leave here." Before Jason could respond, he said to me, "And I have more questions for you to answer, so tell me where—"

"Are you going to arrest me?" Even nonsuspects said that on the TV cop shows.

"Don't act stupid," he said. He handed me his business card. Burton stuck out his hand and took one as well.

"In that case, take this." I handed him my card. "If you want to call, try my cell first. That's the easier way to get me."

He snatched my card and hurried away from us. I thought the action was abrupt, but the phone call may have been the reason. Or maybe that's who Ollie Viktor was and the way he always behaved.

"I must also leave you," Jason said. "I am here in room 300. I take only two breaks during the day. This is my first one, such as I am doing at this moment. I go outside on these grounds so that I may stretch the legs, as you call it." He grinned before he added, "Do I not?"

Burton patted him on the back. "I love your humor."

"And so do I," I said.

"Yes, is it not wonderful to be able to laugh?" Jason shook our hands and hurried away from us past the magnolia tree.

As he left us, I looked at my watch. It was only 11:20. "I know you came here for some kind of spiritual retreat," I said, "but you probably eat lunch. Unless you're here on some kind of fast. Even though it's a little early, would you—"

"Good idea, and you'll be my guest."

"And, Mr. Burton," I said, "I was taught that the person who invites, pays. Or are you going to be one of those old-fashioned macho types who insist—"

"But you didn't ask."

"Was that not implied in my question?" I tried to do my best to imitate Jason Omore's accent and cadence.

He held up both hands. "Surrender. You win. Why don't you buy me lunch?"

He and I turned and started back toward the hotel. His eyes focused on the building, and he obviously counted to the sixth floor. He had been there before, so I assumed he knew where 623 would be.

"Look! Someone's in that room! In 623!"

I followed the direction of his pointing fingers. A woman moved quickly past the window. I recognized her. "It's the widow," I said.

"The who?"

"You met her. The woman with those hideous orange-colored nails?"

He stared at me, frowning.

"Never mind." I grabbed his arm. "Let's go. I don't know how fast I can travel in these heels, so I'm hanging on." Of course, I had another reason to hang on, but that excuse worked.

Burton led me to the elevators, and one of them was open. In less than three minutes, we were outside room 623. The police had not put up one of those yellow ribbons, which I thought was good. Or maybe they only put up yellow crime-scene tape on TV.

I released Burton's arm and rushed ahead. I knocked loudly on the door. "Maid service!"

There was no answer, so I yelled again and tried the knob. "Maid service!"

"Can you come back?" A woman's voice answered.

"Gotta come in now," I said. "No come later." That was my attempt at Hispanic-style English.

A few seconds passed before she opened the door. She glared at me. "You're not the maid!"

"You're not the sentimental widow either!" I said and pushed the door open. Burton and I both stepped inside. "This is the one," I said to Burton. "She claims to be a widow who wanted to visit this room because it was her anniversary. She didn't say she wanted to ransack the room."

"I know this must look bad," she said. "I can explain."

I learned early in my training that silence is a powerful tool. If I waited long enough and said nothing, she would feel obligated to explain. Burton didn't say a word.

"I lied," she said. "I'm a writer. I'm with *Atlanta* magazine. I came here to do a story on Mr. Lauber."

"Mr. Lauber is dead," I said, "so he can't give you any good quotes."

"I wanted information. . .something—something I can use for my article. I'm, uh, going to do a story about his adjustment after prison. . .and, uh, I thought that if I looked in his room. . ." Her cadence had slowed to a complete stop. She must have recognized how implausible her story sounded.

"Hmm," I said. "That story was a pretty good recovery, wasn't it?" I asked Burton.

"Not bad for someone who gets no warning. Want to tell us the truth?" Burton asked softly.

"I think I want to get out of here." She clutched her shoulder bag and turned toward the door. At the first chance, I knew she would rush out of the room. We weren't the police, so we couldn't stop her. Or maybe she thought we were the police.

For the first time, I realized how badly the room had been torn apart. "Did you do all of this?" I tried to sound like someone with authority. "Did your search reveal whatever you wanted?"

"It was already like this when I came. That's the truth." She tried to brush past us, but Burton pulled the door closed behind him.

"Let me go," she said. "Who are you anyway?"

"Who are you?" I asked.

"I told you. . .I—I—"

"You don't work for *Atlanta* magazine," I said. It was one of those intuitive statements that just came out. I have no idea how I knew, but I did.

"I write for them," she said. "I do."

"Do you really?" I asked and refused to look away.

"Okay, twice," she said. "I've sold them two articles."

"So who are you?" Burton asked.

"That's not important."

"You want the diamonds," I said, again an intuitive statement.

"Okay, I want them. Who doesn't? We all knew Stefan had them."

"Who is *we*?" Burton asked.

Instead of answering, she grabbed the door handle and pulled the door open. She raced out of the room. The quick tapping of her feet retreated down the hallway.

"What was that all about?" Burton asked.

"I don't know," I said, "but let's go to lunch and talk about it."

"How did she get into the room?" he asked. "You

tried the door and it was locked."

I had wondered, as well. "That means she probably had a key and still has it with her." I looked around.

"I don't believe she would have put it down in all this mess."

"I think I know how she got it," I said. "Let's go back to the front desk."

Burton snapped his fingers. "Of course!"

That man is quick and bright. In fact, I'm surprised he didn't think of it before I did.

As soon as we got off the elevator, we walked to the front desk. I gave Craig my best smile and said softly, "How much did she pay you for the key to 623?"

He blinked several times. I could all but see the wheels scurrying around in his brain as he wondered whether he should deny or admit the bribe. "Uh."

"Never mind," Burton said. "You've answered the question. We wanted to know how she got access to the room. You've just told us."

"Please don't report me," he said. "She came back right after you walked away with the detective. She begged me."

"And I suppose fifty dollars helped," I said.

"It was only forty. I don't care what she said. That's all she gave me."

"I won't tell," I said. I took Burton's arm, and we moved away and toward the hallway leading to the dining room.

We walked into the elegant dining room, its walls papered with a soft gold and brown pattern. The ornate tables and chairs looked like something stolen from a *Masterpiece Theatre* set.

"I am sorry, but you are too early for lunch," the maître d' said with a slight Hispanic accent. "But if you can be accommodated with tea, I could serve you while you wait, or you might choose to return in twenty minutes."

"Tea is fine," Burton said, and we followed the maître d' to a table by the window. It faced the east, and I could see wisteria vines that had been snaking their way up the side of the building for the past three or four decades. I don't like their fragrance, but I love the soft, purplish flowers.

A matronly waitress in a black dress and white apron brought in two bone china cups and saucers and a tall delft teapot on a tray. Without being asked, Burton slipped into the role of host for the tea ceremony. He checked the pot for "nose," and with tiny silver tongs, he placed thinly sliced lemon in both cups before he poured in the pale golden liquid. He held up the milk, and I shook my head. He looked up and smiled. "I lived in England for a year," he said.

"Very nice." I wanted him to feel I didn't know anything, although I had lived with an aristocratic British family for nearly two years. I had been a nanny to their sweet-tempered boy. And he truly was easy to take care of. If he hadn't been, I probably wouldn't have lasted the two years while I did my graduate studies.

Burton reviewed what little we knew about the late Stefan Lauber, which wasn't much. Both of us seemed surprised that he wanted me to be the courier to return the diamonds.

"Why me?" I asked for at least the fifth time. "I hardly knew him."

"He trusted you. That's what Jason Omore said." Burton took a long sip of his tea. "Don't give me one of your smart responses." He smiled. "Stefan Lauber obviously grasped what a fine and trustworthy person you are."

I stared at Burton for several seconds. "That's probably one of the nicest things you've ever said to me." I wanted to hug him and let him hold me in his arms, but that wasn't appropriate considering the place and the status of our relationship. But a woman can daydream, can't she?

We finished tea, and I tried to think of what to say next to keep him around.

"This time I do need to leave you," Burton said before I could think of something clever, "but it's nice to see you again." Like the gentleman he was, Burton waited for me to move first before he got out of his chair and slipped behind to assist me. I left enough cash on the table for the tea and a generous tip.

We reached the front desk just as the phone rang. Craig cried out, "Okay, okay. Be calm." And his voice was anything but calm.

"We'll call 911. Right now!" He opened the door to the inner office and yelled to some unseen person, "Cover for me. It's room 623! Again!"

He pulled out his cell phone and was so focused on the emergency that when he rushed around the counter, he collided with Burton. "Sorry. It's that room again—that 623!" He began to run. On the cell we heard him say, "This is the Cartledge Inn. It's room

623 again." He said something else, but he was too far ahead of us for me to understand the words.

This time Burton grabbed my arm and propelled me toward the elevator. We moved faster than the clerk, passed him, and reached the elevator before he did. I pressed the button. In the seconds before the elevator arrived, the harried clerk shook his head and said, "Murder. It's another murder."

"What?" I said.

"That's what the maid just said. She's up there yelling and crying."

The elevator arrived, and Burton punched the button for the sixth floor. When we got off, we hurried down to the room. A Hispanic maid stood outside the door. Her body shook, and she cried loudly, mixing her Spanish and her English. "Dead! *Ella está muerta!* Murdered. *Matado!* On the floor!"

A second maid, an Asian, stood calmly on the other side of her cart. "There. In that way. The door was open—very wide open—and both of us saw her."

The clerk started to rush inside, but Burton held him back. "Don't take a single step into the room." He unclipped his cell and pulled Ollie's card out of his pocket. He dialed the detective. "Get back to the hotel. There's a dead woman in room 623."

While Burton talked to the detective, I moved to the door and surveyed the room. I saw the body—I couldn't miss it. It was the woman we had seen in the room before, the one with those outrageous burnt orange nails. I wasn't ready to look closely at her, so I scanned the room. It was even more torn apart than it had been when Burton and I had been there less than an hour earlier. The air vent near the ceiling had been pulled out and tossed carelessly on top of the torn-up bed. The wooden headboard for the bed had been ripped from the wall. The mattress was flipped over. I was surprised it wasn't cut open—they do that in the movies, which always seemed silly to me. The three drawers of the bedside stand had been thrown across the room. The intruder had pulled out the clothes that had once hung inside an old-fashioned armoire made of real oak. One of the doors was ripped off its hinges. Everything indicated that the search had been done in a fit of rage.

Finally it was time to look at the body. I stared, mute. She lay on her back. Another shooting. I'm no expert, but it looked as if she had been shot in the chest and the bullet went through her. Most of the blood seeped from beneath her.

At first I wondered why someone didn't hear the noise, but perhaps there had been no one around. It was, after all, midday, and most guests were out of their rooms.

"Who is she really?" Burton asked. "She lied to us once."

"Even then she didn't tell us her name," I said. "But when she registered, she did use a credit card—"

"So who was she?" Burton asked the clerk.

"I'm still so rattled, I don't remember the name," Craig said.

"I know who she is." I turned around. A tall woman said, "Her name is Deedra Knight. At least that's the name I knew her by."

5

Before I had a chance to question the woman, she stepped into the doorway of room 623 and said, "I haven't seen Deedra for years, but she hasn't changed much. She still has those cheap-looking acrylic nails. Frankly, from the back side she looks better than she ever did from the front."

"And who are you?"

"My name is Janet *Lauber* Grand, and before you ask, I didn't like her. In fact, I detested her."

"Well, at least we know who she is," I said. "I mean, who she was."

"And you're with the police, is that correct?" She glared at me. I said nothing, and she quickly picked up on that. "You're not, are you? So why *are* you here?"

I stared at her, but I couldn't see the faintest family resemblance. Instead of answering her question, I asked, "How did you know which room was Stefan's?"

"First, because he called me on the phone yesterday and said he was now staying at this inn. Second, I have no idea who you are and why you're asking me these questions. You are not with the police, are you?"

"No," I said.

"Third, perhaps you ought to explain to me. Stefan was my brother. After I learned he had passed, I came. . .well, I came to see if there was anything, you know, anything I could do."

"Where did you come from?" Burton asked. "How did you know to come to this room?"

"I walked toward the reception desk. I came in through the side parking lot. I heard this man," she said, pointing to Craig, "shouting in a most unprofessional manner. Something about another murder in room 623." She explained that by the time she reached the elevator, it had closed, so she watched the dial above the elevator, saw that it stopped on the sixth floor, and rang for the second elevator. "When I came off the elevator, I saw you three standing in front of this door. Now, *who are you?*"

"I'm the desk clerk," Craig said.

"I don't mean *you*." The contempt was heavy in her voice. "With that blazer and your name on the jacket, that is patently obvious. I mean these two."

"I'm a therapist," I said and told her that Stefan had asked me to come to see him.

"A therapist? Stefan with a psychiatrist? You must be joking."

I'm a psychologist, but I didn't correct her.

"She isn't joking," Burton said and introduced himself.

"And now you're going to tell me that my brother decided to study for the priesthood."

"I never met your brother," Burton said. "I'm a guest at the hotel."

"Then what right do you have to ask me anything?" she said. "I'm not going to tell you anything more."

"Then tell *me*."

I jumped and turned around. None of us had heard Ollie Viktor come into the room.

He held up his badge and waved it in front of the woman.

"In that case, I'm delighted to talk to someone who obviously has the authority to ask questions." She gave me a half-second smile that wasn't worth moving her facial muscles. She turned to Ollie, eyed him, and nodded in approval of either his general appearance or his good looks. "My name is Mrs. Janet *Lauber* Grand." She accented *Lauber* again. "Stefan was my brother." She tilted her chin. "My much older brother."

I wouldn't have believed it, but she was flirting with Ollie, smiling and fawning, and she moved around so he could see her trim figure. Okay, she was beautiful— even I had to admit that much. She was also a woman who had been around—a lot. The hardness in her eyes and the tautness around her mouth were two things her expensive makeup couldn't hide. Her face, which seemed tightened regularly by a plastic surgeon to retain its youth, was expertly made up, as if she were about to walk on stage or on a runway. Her iridescent blond hair curled softly and stopped just below her ears. I suppose that was to cover any signs of the surgeon's knife. She wore off-white cashmere slacks and a silk blouse of the same color. She probably spent more on that outfit than I laid out for a full wardrobe. Around her neck and on her wrists and fingers she displayed a great many diamonds.

Ollie stared at her jewelry.

"You like this? It's my daytime wear," she said and rewarded him with a generous smile. "You are so very observant."

"How could he miss it?" I wanted to say but held my mouth shut.

"And you came to this room because. . ." Ollie asked.

"Because—because I heard my brother's name shouted—quite loudly, as a matter of fact—by the desk clerk."

"I did not mention his name!" Craig said.

She waved him to silence and sighed deeply. From her purse she took a silk handkerchief that matched her blouse. It reeked of gardenias. She sniffed a few times and wiped her eyes as if tears had fallen. She wasn't a great actress, but she was pretty good. Most men probably fell for her performance. I wondered if that was why she had so many jewels.

"I'm sorry you have to go through this emotional ordeal," Ollie said. That was the softest I had heard him speak. Maybe a real heart beat inside his chest after all. Or maybe he had just been overwhelmed by her obvious attention.

"I didn't know—I didn't know he—what to do—Stefan was my brother—and I wanted to do something—anything during our time of deep grief." She handled that line extremely well. She not only used the Southern expressions, but her drawl was so good I expected honeysuckle to drip from her fingers. "I didn't know until I heard the desk clerk—"

"I'm sorry," Craig said with contriteness written across his face. "I was excited and—"

Ollie waved him to silence. "Go on back to your desk," he said and moved out of the way so Craig could get past him.

Ollie turned to Burton. "I got your call just as I pulled into the parking lot. The team will be here in a few minutes." He pushed past me as if I didn't exist, walked the few feet into the room, and knelt beside the woman's body. "So who is she?"

"Deedra Knight," I said. "Or so she says." I nodded toward Janet.

"Any of you know what she was doing in this room?"

"Obviously searching for. . ." Janet paused and added, "For—for something. It must be something of immense value. Why, just look at this terrible chaos." She put her hand to her face, and I thought she did that better than Vivien Leigh in the old film *Streetcar Named Desire*. Next I'd expect her to dim the lights in the room because they were too harsh on her face.

"The room was in disorder from before," Ollie said. He paused and looked around. "Maybe not quite this much of a mess when we arrived last night." He turned to face me. "I was here last night just before the uniformed officers left."

I gave him my best dumb-little-me smile.

"So you think people—someone—is looking for the diamonds?" Burton asked.

"Maybe. My supervisor doesn't think so—"

"But you felt he had them—even before Jason said anything."

"Yeah."

"Because—"

"Professional intuition," he said.

"So did you look?" Burton asked. "I mean, last night, did you—"

Ollie nodded. "They weren't on his person, and the two officers who searched last night didn't find anything of value inside this room. It was already a mess when they came, so they tried to be careful not to disturb any evidence."

"So the point is," Janet said, leaning against the doorjamb as if posing for a photo shoot, "you did not find anything that belonged to my dear, dearly departed brother."

"What they searched for didn't belong to your dear, dearly departed brother." I think my accent was almost as good as hers. Burton's slight shaking of his head begged me to stop poking fun at her. "They were stolen diamonds."

"And at least we're fairly sure the first searchers didn't find them or there would have been no second murder," Ollie said. I'm not sure what a man looks like when he preens, but that's how I'd describe the way he straightened his shoulders. "Yeah, this second murder and more destruction probably says the second search didn't yield anything either."

"Or the person found it and stopped the search," I added.

"You may be correct," Ollie said. "But for now we'll go on the assumption they have not found the diamonds."

"And the diamonds the other gentleman mentioned?" Janet's eyes widened as if she were portraying shock in a silent flick. "Surely you don't mean the diamonds from that utterly terrible, terrible robbery that—"

"That's the one," Ollie said.

"You never found them?"

"No, ma'am, we never did," Ollie said. "They're worth a lot of money, and we'd sure like to recover them. That's not the reason for the investigation. This started purely as a murder—"

"And you just happened to tie him in with the diamonds?" I asked.

"Not until we ran his name through our computer." He shrugged. "I returned to look over the scene, but there seemed no hard evidence to connect him to any diamonds—"

"Until Jason Omore said something. Right?" I asked.

"Yes, that's correct," Ollie said. "I thought I'd look this over one more time before I reported—"

"I had no idea, absolutely no idea the diamonds were still missing." Janet Grand really laid it on thick. As I watched her, I sensed she was lying about being Stefan's sister. I kept trying to remember what Stefan had said about his family of origin. He had an ex-wife and admitted to having affairs with several women. Was she one of those women? The more I observed Janet Grand—if that was her name—the more she seemed to fit into that category.

"Can you prove that you're his sister?" I asked.

She turned her back on me and faced Ollie. "I shall be delighted to answer any questions you have for me." She sighed deeply again. "But please, only questions from you."

"This is a police matter," Ollie said. "You don't belong here—"

"But we're here," Burton said. "I hope we can be of help. We'll stay out of the way." He looked at me. "Won't we?"

Instead of making a rude remark and getting another shake of the head from Burton, I interrupted, "Did you notice the connecting door?" I motioned toward the door that led to 625. "It's all but closed." I tiptoed past Miss Mint Julep and pointed to the bottom of the door. "See?" It was a fraction away from being closed.

Ollie walked over to the door. He didn't exactly push me out of the way. Or maybe he did, but I assumed he was focused on the door. He reached forward to pull it when he must have realized that it pushed inward toward 625. So he nudged it and the door swung open. Because I stood near him, I could see inside. It hadn't been torn up like 623. It looked like any other upscale hotel room to me. I knew it was occupied, because I spotted a small stack of books on the desk in the corner.

Ollie turned back to all of us and held up his right hand. I was sure he'd seen that done on TV, because he was just too perfect at it. "Just stay where you are." He walked around inside 625. I couldn't see everything, but I heard him pick up the phone and punch a number. "This is Detective Viktor upstairs. Who is registered in room 625?"

After a lengthy pause, he asked, "Do you have a phone number for his office? A cell number?" He muttered something, and I heard the rumble of his voice for a full minute or so before he replaced the phone.

After he returned to the room, he spread his arms out to usher us into the hallway. "What do you say we all go downstairs and find a quiet place so we can talk?"

"Who's in room 625?" I asked.

He smiled. "Let's go downstairs. All four of us."

Obviously he wasn't going to tell us, so we let him direct us away from the room and down the hallway.

No one said a word until we got back to the main floor. Ollie told us to wait while he left us and spoke to Craig. I had remained focused on Janet.

"How long has it been since you last saw your brother?"

"Awhile."

"How long is that?"

"I prefer not to discuss this, especially with you. The pain is already so—so intense." She pulled ahead of me and stood next to Ollie.

"Follow me," Ollie said and waved toward us. He led us to the end of the reception area, and we made a left turn and entered a small room. It had already been set up for a business meeting with a whiteboard and memo pads and pens in front of every chair. Every table had two pitchers of ice water and a stack of glasses. PowerPoint equipment was ready for whoever had booked the room. "Desk clerk says this room is free for about an hour." He tried to smile, and maybe he actually did, but it looked forced. "Sit down."

"Let's start with you," he said and focused on Janet. He took out his little notebook, thumbed through several pages, and wrote on a new page. "Tell us about Deedra Knight."

She shrugged as if she felt confused. Again she touched her cheek with her right hand, and the large diamond on her ring finger sparkled. "She was. . .I think the word is. . .Stefan's coliguillas."

"No, a coliguillas is a man," I said gleefully, using the proper Spanish pronunciation. "You probably mean something old-fashioned such as *courtesan*. Doxy, maybe? Or perhaps—"

"Enough of that, Doc," Ollie said to me. "Just let the lady speak."

If I had thought about it, I would have given him an Ollie-type shrug, but instead I nodded. I really wanted to hear her myself.

"She was, uh, I suppose what I mean is that she was intimate with both my brother and Willie Petersen. She played them both. This is conjecture, of course, but from what I know of her and of Stefan's past, it fits. She also had something to do with the robbery. In fact, Stefan once hinted that she was the one who set it up." For a second her mask fell as she realized she'd told us more than she was supposed to have known. "By that I mean Stefan never said anything about a robbery, but he did mention a big business situation in which he was closely involved. And then, of course, he was arrested and sent to prison."

"And why do you think Deedra had anything to do with that?" I asked.

Her contemptuous glare should have made me back down, but it only pushed me to pursue the question.

"You seem to know a great deal for a person who supposedly knows nothing," I said. I didn't know what I meant, but it sounded good to my own ears.

"I know little," she said and faced Ollie. "In fact, I know almost nothing." She paused as if embarrassed, but I figured she did that for dramatic effect. "You do understand that I am telling you only what I assume is true. Everything I have said or could add would be purely conjecture."

"I had understood your brother was the one who

planned this," I said. I wanted to push on about that matter.

"I doubt that." She still refused to look at me. "It was not the sort of ugly, evil thing he would have done."

"As his therapist, I can say with authority that he planned the robbery." Again, I have no idea where that statement came from and hoped no one would push me. That woman was lying—probably about everything.

"If you choose to think so, but I can assure you that—that horrible woman—that Deedra Knight originated it. Stefan was so easily influenced by. . .uh, by women of sordid reputations."

"Oh, really?" I had to throw that one in.

"Neither man—Stefan nor Willie—would have done such a thing without being goaded by her." She leaned toward the detective. "You believe me, don't you?"

Ollie nodded before he flipped a page in his notebook and jotted down a number of items. He kept his left hand over the page so I couldn't see the script.

"So why do you think Deedra came here?" he asked.

"Wasn't it obvious?"

Obvious? In what way?" Ollie Viktor asked.

"To search for the diamonds. Didn't you say as much?"

He shrugged. So we were back to that gesture. "What else can you tell me?"

"Nothing. I'm sure. I don't know anything. I came to see my brother. That was the sole purpose for the visit." She pulled out the off-white handkerchief again and held it to her dry eyes. She must have practiced that before a mirror, because she did it exactly the same way again.

"I have some interesting news for you," Ollie said. "Your other brother is also a guest in this place. What's his name?"

"Lucas? Lucas is here? In this hotel?"

"He's checked into room 625. He may have been one of the people who wanted 623 but couldn't get it."

"Lucas and I haven't spoken in years, and it has nothing to do with this matter. We stopped speaking more than twenty years ago." She smiled and added, "I was willing to forgive him, but he refused to apologize for his—his bad behavior."

"Do you have any idea why he's here?"

She shook her head. "None." She stood up. "I must go. I have an important appointment. If my brother is not alive, there is nothing here for me, is there?"

"Don't you want to see Lucas?"

"Absolutely not," she said.

"Perhaps the mutual grief would unite you," I said.

"Perhaps you ought to stay out of things that do not concern you."

Before I could conjure up a rejoinder, Burton shook his head, and she had reached the door.

Ollie stopped her and asked for her address and phone number. He said he'd let her know if he learned anything else.

"Now I need to get back to you," Ollie said and glared at me. "This morning you were ready to tell me about your sessions with the victim."

"You mean my sessions with Stefan Lauber?" Okay, that was evasive and out of line, but I didn't like him, and I wasn't going to make it any easier.

"When we spoke this morning, there was only one victim." Although his voice hadn't changed, his fist had knotted and his eyes showed agitation. I decided to push him to see how upset he would become with me. At the same time, I wondered how he ever solved crimes if he was so impatient.

"Yes, of course," I said. Just that one question and his impatience was already showing.

"What do you want to know about our sessions?" I leaned slightly forward. "Do you want his personal history? His romantic secrets? His—"

He slammed his fist on the table. "Don't be cute or coy. I don't give a dead man's noose about his personal life. Stop being evasive. I want to know why he came to see you."

"Just that?"

"Yes. That's a simple question, isn't it?"

I hesitated, not sure how much to say. Burton leaned close and said softly, "Tell him. This isn't you and me at Palm Island trying to solve a murder. He's the professional here."

Although I like Burton, a brusque retort formed in my mind. But he was right. I didn't like the detective, but he was the professional. "Okay, I'll tell you," I said. "First, of course, Janet isn't his sister. I don't know who she is, but Stefan had no sister." I hoped he wouldn't ask me to prove that, but the feeling was so strong, I trusted my intuition.

"You're sure about that?" Burton said. "Maybe we need to stop her."

Ollie leaned back in his chair. "Very good, Julie, but I already knew that. Stefan was an only child until his parents adopted Lucas, who was five or six years older."

"You knew that?" I was surprised.

"Yes. I also know the reason for the adoption. The parents felt Stefan had gotten unruly and that an older brother was what he needed." He met my gaze. "Is that correct?"

"For a man who has no direct interest in this case," I said, "you certainly know a great deal."

"Computers. Everything's on computers these days," he said.

"I didn't know about the adoption, although I knew the brothers didn't get along. That was one of the issues Stefan talked about. After they were both grown, he cheated Lucas out of a large sum of money—"

"About a hundred grand," the detective said.

"If you know all this—"

"So far you haven't told me anything new, but you will." He poured himself a glass of water and gulped it down in one long swallow. "I'm still listening. A little impatiently, but I am listening."

"Did you get all that information from computers?" I asked. "Wow, what's the URL?"

"Julie." Burton spoke my name softly, but I knew he wanted me to back off.

"I'm not giving information now. I'm receiving it."

"Okay, then what about that woman—Janet Grand?" I asked.

"I know who she is. She was one of those—how did she say it?—intimate people with Stefan. Somehow she found out about the murder and knew about the diamonds."

"Really?" Burton asked.

"She tried to book the room by phone this morning—about an hour before she showed up." He smiled as if to say, *"See, I'm ahead of you on his case."*

Even though Stefan was dead, I didn't feel comfortable telling the detective anything. My intuition said he wasn't a man I could trust. Or maybe that was only my prejudice. Maybe I just didn't like him as a person—which I didn't—and that may have distorted my reasoning. Besides, he was so different from his college classmate, and I had as low an opinion of him as I had a high one of Burton.

"I didn't know about any religious experience he may have had," I said. "Or his *conversion,* as Jason Omore called it. That's not an area we talked about. However, I knew something had happened—something that changed him. When he first came to me, he told me, quite up front, that he had a number of unresolved issues in his life and said he wanted to change." I paused, shrugged to imitate Ollie, and plunged on. "Actually, he said it even stronger. He said he was determined to change."

Ollie threw more questions at me. Each time, he wrote something in his little book and must have flipped six or seven pages. I wondered if they had to buy those things themselves. They must use a lot of them.

I asked Ollie to give me a couple of minutes to review my professional relationship with Stefan. I didn't need that reflection time, but I wanted to see if he'd push me to hurry.

He said nothing, but it was obvious he didn't like the silence. While I reflected, his fingers drummed on the table.

"I saw him a total of six times," I said.

"Yeah, okay," Ollie said.

I got up, walked to the far side of the room, stalling for time, unsure of how much I wanted to tell him.

"Any day now," Ollie said.

"Yes, there were six sessions. The first time, a Monday afternoon, not much went on, mostly his giving me information about himself. He did speak of significant issues in his life and said he was trying to figure out the right thing to do.

"He refused to say more except that he wanted to be sure he could trust me before he went into details. We set a second appointment for Thursday of the same week. Ordinarily I don't do two appointments in the same week, but he had insisted, and I felt he was nearing a crisis stage about something. I agreed."

I lapsed into silence again, wanting to think about how much to say. By the middle of the second session, he had begun to trust me. I can always tell when that happens. It's not just the way the clients talk, but their bodies relax and their voices grow softer. At the first session, Stefan had sat tall, straight, and stiff. During the second session, he relaxed, and for the second half of his appointment time, he sat in my office with legs wide apart and arms stretched across the back of the couch.

I decided to omit whatever I didn't want to tell Ollie. I walked back to my chair and said, "Okay, I have it sorted out."

"At last," Ollie muttered.

I ignored that. "Okay, what you need to know is that Stefan cheated several people," I said. "His brother was only the first. That was some kind of obscure business deal. Stefan didn't go into detail, other than to say he did it and his brother found out—and he wasn't supposed to know. When Lucas heard, he vowed to kill Stefan."

"Hmm. Really?" Ollie said and scribbled hurriedly on the pad.

"That happened long ago, you see, and I don't know if—"

"Some family feuds can last a long time," he said. "Go on."

"Stefan never mentioned the diamond robbery, but he hinted. I mean, in retrospect, it seems to fit. Several times he referred to himself as the big kahuna—"

"The big guy, the top dog," Ollie said. "It's a Hawaiian term—"

"So you also saw all those dumb beach movies," I said.

Ollie blushed. He actually blushed when I said that. I liked him a little for that unconscious act—not a lot better, but somewhat.

"Yes, any number of times he said that he had become the big kahuna with a brilliant idea that had gone wrong. Now I can see that's what he meant. He said he had been involved in something illegal and dangerous and people got hurt—something for which he had never planned."

"That was as specific as he got?"

"Pretty much," I said.

"And?" Ollie prompted.

"During our third or fourth session, he asked pointedly because he wanted to be certain: 'Please assure me that, no matter what I tell you in these sessions, you cannot be compelled to testify against me in court.' I told him not only that it was true, but that he already knew that."

"How did he answer?" Burton asked.

"He said he needed to know for his own peace of mind."

"So I guess he didn't trust you," Ollie said. "Is that it?"

I stared at him for a moment and then closed my eyes and rethought that session. "No, I don't think so. In fact, I think it was an odd, perhaps subtle way of affirming that he felt he could trust me."

"Doesn't sound like it to me."

"That's why I'm the professional." I said the words quietly, but from the corner of my eye I saw Burton's head shake slightly. Who appointed Burton to be my conscience? Okay, maybe I did, and he was right.

"Okay, sorry for that," I said. "He admitted that

it was for his own peace of mind. This may not make sense to you, Detective, but in my professional assessment, Stefan wanted me to say *out loud* that anything and everything he said in our sessions was privileged communication. It was almost as if he did that for the benefit of anyone who might be listening. And, of course, I never tape such sessions. But then, perhaps, his having been in prison—"

"Perhaps he taped *you*," Burton said.

"If he did, I never saw a recorder anywhere," I said. "But that thought went through my mind at the time. However, it didn't matter. If he had asked, I would have allowed him to tape any sessions—"

"Okay, let's move on, please," Ollie said. "Tomorrow will be here before you tell me anything significant."

I gave what I assumed was a warm and apologetic smile before I said, "Stefan told me he wanted to make full restitution for his crimes. Those were his exact words: full restitution for his crimes."

"Did he say what his crimes were?" Ollie leaned forward as he asked.

I ignored his question. I had decided to tell him, but it would be in my own way. "Stefan didn't look like the kind of person I would consider a criminal." I laughed at myself. "Okay, he was, but he didn't act like one. He had none of the signs." I turned to Burton for help.

He nodded slowly before he said, "I understand, and I think Ollie does, too."

"Okay, he didn't give off any bad vibes. He was a genteel, reformed criminal," Ollie said.

"And if he had changed," Burton said, "if he had

become born again, surely that would have made him behave differently."

"Yes, I suppose it would," I said and knew my words didn't sound very convincing, because I wasn't sure his conversion—or whatever he had experienced—was relevant. I had met a number of the born-again types and—okay, I don't want to digress and go on that diatribe. "I can say that he seemed to be genuinely honest and a man who was determined to grow." I leaned forward to match Ollie's posture. I also wanted him to know the sincerity of my client—my former client. "He listened to everything I said. He probed within his own heart. At times it was painful, but he faced things about himself—his personal values and attitudes. He was definitely committed to change."

"Change in what way?" Ollie said. "To make restitution sounds good, but you still haven't told me anything new."

"He mentioned the names of several people he had hurt. They're names I know now. He referred to Deedra—by first name only—and someone named Willie and his brother, Lucas. There was also another woman, but he never mentioned her name. His struggle, so far as I could figure out, was how he could right the wrongs he had done with his business associates—again, that was his terminology—through his illegal actions and yet make things right so that he could live with himself."

"And you believed him?" Burton asked. "You believed he spoke the truth?"

"Absolutely," I said. "I've been at this profession too long to have been taken in."

Ollie snorted, and I gave him my most intense glare.

"Okay, okay, you believed him," Ollie said. "And?"

"Stefan felt that if he made things right with the people he had hurt and gave them what they insisted they deserved, it would be an immoral act. If he didn't make things right with them, he felt it would not be ethical for him." I paused and thought back to his words. "He may have used the word *God* once or twice. People often do, but they don't usually mean divine power or anything like that."

"Do you think he meant *God*?" Burton asked.

"Not at the time I didn't," I said. "But after our conversation today with Jason, I think he probably did."

"Okay, okay," Ollie said. "I don't care. You're holding back on me, aren't you?"

"Okay, it's like this. Stefan wanted to make everybody happy, and he knew he couldn't do that," I said.

"How could he make everyone happy?" The detective looked at me. "What was he trying to do? Become some kind of saint?"

"I don't know. I can only tell you what he told me—"

"As well as a few of your insights," Burton said.

"That, too. Stefan continually asked himself one question—"

"What question?" Ollie asked.

Ollie was impatient. I paused, stared at him, and finally said, "Please. You asked me to tell you what I know, so don't constantly interrupt."

"Yeah, okay, but just get on with it."

"Stefan had several things to resolve, but what troubled him the most was the one question he would ask aloud. By asking, he didn't mean he wanted me to give him the answer—"

"Then why did he ask?" Ollie interjected. Aware of what he had done, he looked away.

"Some people need to talk aloud. They need to say the words to another person before they know what they think. Make sense?" I got a slight nod from Burton and a blank stare from Ollie. "Here's the way I say it: I only know of myself what I say of myself. That means I don't really know how I feel about something until I say it to someone else."

"Yeah? What good does that do?" the questioner interrupted yet again.

"Two things take place," I said. I decided to act gracious and ignore his impatience. "First, and in this case, Stefan was able to put his emotions into words. In our field we say that when a person like Stefan feels safe—feels understood and trusts the therapist—he'll speak from his heart. Things come up that he might not otherwise say."

"Okay, I get that. So what's the second?"

This detective would provide a great venture for a team of therapists. Besides his impatience, I sensed his high level of anxiety. "Are you always so intense and so. . .anxiety-ridden as you are now?" I asked him.

He opened his mouth, and I think he was going to swear at me, but he glared at Burton and said, "Look. This isn't about me, and I didn't hire you to be my personal shrink, okay? Just tell me about Lauber. You may be a good therapist, but it sure takes you a long time to get to the point!" His voice had raised in pitch, and he stood up. He mumbled something about being sorry but he was eager to solve the case.

"Eager or anxious?" I asked.

Ollie stared blankly.

"Okay, I'll let that go," I said. I actually enjoyed watching his responses. He might be a hunk, but his wires were so tight they were ready to snap. "Stefan sat in front of me, often leaning forward, his head down, and he would say, 'What is the right thing to do?' He didn't ask that just once, but repeatedly: 'What is the right thing to do?' "

"The right thing about what?" Ollie asked.

"He didn't say. As a therapist, I didn't feel I needed to probe for that. He knew. That's what counted." I scooted forward until our heads were only about three feet apart. "You question people all the time, don't you?"

He nodded.

"But you do it to elicit information. Correct?"

"What else?"

I held up my hand. "That's not how a therapist works." I turned to Burton for help, not because I couldn't express myself, but because I sensed Ollie would listen to his old friend.

"I think she's trying to say that she wasn't probing. There is a time to probe—a time when a therapist asks the questions that open people up and enable them to get in touch with their deeper selves—their inner child or their—"

"Okay, okay, I think I get it."

"I'm not sure you do," I said. "He had already

begun to open up. I sensed the trust level was high. Once that happened, my role was to allow him to work out the problems by himself. Instead of trying to hand him answers—"

"More psychobabble!"

"Not really," Burton said. He gently laid his hand on Ollie's shoulder. "She's trying to explain how this works. She's saying that Stefan had to resolve the problem himself. Her role was to remain objective, to be open to listening, and to encourage him so that he kept moving forward."

"Very good," I said. I wanted to hug Burton for that. But then, I wanted to hug him for a variety of reasons.

"Okay, I get it," Ollie said. "I ask to get information. You ask to get a person to look inward. I understand, and now I've passed Psych 101. Now, Dr. West, what else can you tell me?" He spoke softly, but the words were uttered as if he were ready to sock my jaw.

"He said nothing directly about the robbery or the diamonds; however, from what I've heard since I've been here, I think he wanted to return the diamonds to their rightful owners."

"That's a consortium based here in Atlanta," Ollie said. "I'm sure that long ago, however, the insurance paid for the loss, so I don't know how that works. That's not the issue anyway."

"The issue was his dilemma of trying to figure out the right action," I said, "and how to do that so he hurt the fewest number of people."

"But he had the diamonds. Right?"

"How should I know?" I asked, but I added, "Yeah, probably."

Ollie's cell phone buzzed again. He held up his hand for me to wait, which was quite unnecessary. I didn't want to say anything more, and I did want to hear what he had to say on the phone.

"You're kidding me!" Ollie said, followed by a series of one-word responses. "Was he obsessed with that number?" Those were the two longest statements he made before he hung up.

I raised my eyebrows as my silent way to ask Ollie to share information with us.

"You're both in the head-and-heart business," he said. He still held his cell and turned it over and over in his hand. "So maybe you can help us with this one. It's the number 623. That Lauber was obsessed with 623. Weird, huh?"

"Obsessed?" I asked.

"Yes," he said and raised his right index finger. "First, he lives here in room 623. He's been here for months. Second," and he held up another finger, "he rented post office box 623 in Stone Mountain and also box 623 at Decatur's main post office." He now held up three fingers.

"That's certainly odd," Burton said.

"Fourth, he bought a house on Royal Path Court in Decatur. He hadn't moved in because construction isn't finished. It's a tract of land that will eventually have eight houses. His is the only one that's almost finished. They plan to finish the others before the end of the year. His house won't be finished for another month or so. But guess what the number of Lauber's house will be?"

"Another 623?" I asked.

Ollie genuinely smiled. "And even crazier, he bought the first of eight large homes, and all the others—all eight—had already been assigned addresses, and all of them were four digits, but he insisted on his being 623 and said he didn't care what any of the others were."

"How could he do that?" Burton asked. "The builder doesn't assign—"

"He paid cash. Then he turned around and bought the other seven houses as well. He spent 5.3 mil for the entire tract of completed houses. For California that might be nothing, but here in Georgia, that's a big, big hunk of cash."

"For money like that," Burton said, "I guess he could get what he wanted."

"What's the compulsion about 623?" I asked. "Those three digits don't mean anything to me. What about his birthday? Is it possibly 6/23—June twenty-third?"

Ollie shook his head. "His birthday is November something."

"Was he born in 1962 perhaps? That would account for the 62." But I knew the answer. "Too old. He was in his late thirties, wasn't he?"

"Thirty-seven," Ollie said.

We batted around various possibilities for the number for a while, but nothing seemed to make sense.

"One more thing I'll tell you," Ollie said, "but it goes no further than this room. Right?" He stared first at Burton and waited for him to say yes before he turned to me. I nodded my agreement.

Ollie got up and paced the circumference of the small room three or four times. "There is one more thing that might have some value." Ollie told us he had been the first detective to arrive at the inn. The two uniformed officers touched nothing but waited at the door until he arrived. "When I turned over Lauber's body last night, his right hand clutched a piece of paper—more a fragment of a piece—ragged, but only about the bottom two inches. I don't know what happened to the rest of it, but it fits in with this."

"You mean the number 623?" I asked. "It was on the fragment?"

"Yes, and just above it a capital *R* and a small *o*—as in the word *room*. That was printed from a computer, and his handwritten signature was below those two letters."

"What does that tell you?" Burton asked.

"Room 623," he said. "What else?"

For a few seconds I tried to figure out what else would fit. Nothing came to mind. Burton seemed as puzzled as I did.

"I thought maybe you two could add some insight to that." He rubbed the back of his head. "This obsession with 623 is nuts. Just plain nuts."

"Prison cell?" I asked.

He shook his head. "Good thinking, but I checked on that this morning. No connection. In fact, another detective went to the prison and asked around, trying to find some meaning to 623. He came up blank."

For perhaps two minutes more, the three of us sat in silence. Ollie poured himself a second glass of water. The ice had melted, and I wondered if the water would be cold enough for the group that was supposed to use the room a little later.

I decided to stretch as I pondered the situation. I walked to the large windows and looked outside. I admired the cerulean hue of the cloudless sky as it contrasted with the hydrangea along the small path that wound from the sidewalk to the lake. The hydrangea bushes were a bright purple or a soft pink—my dad said the color had something to do with the amount of aluminum in the soil.

I stood in silence; Ollie paced; Burton stared at the ceiling. Just then, the soft noise of the air-conditioning kicked in.

"Is it a code?" Burton asked. "You know, where each number is a letter?"

"Okay, suppose it is," Ollie said. "If 1 is *A* and *B* is 2, that means 6 is *G*, and that gives us GBC. Does GBC mean anything?"

"Or he may have used a different base," I said. "Instead of 1 equals *A*." Then I laughed. "It's just as confusing to try to figure that out as it is to stay with 623. After all, if we want to make sense of what went on inside Stefan's head, we need to understand those three numbers and keep them in that order."

We all agreed.

Aside from the low, indistinct sound of air moving into the room, there was no noise. Ollie reached for a fresh pitcher of water. He poured and gulped down a third glass.

"Something has been bothering me," I said. "It's something Craig, the desk clerk, said."

"What was that?" Burton asked.

"When that woman—Deedra Knight or whoever she was—came to the desk and asked for 623, Craig told her it was taken—"

"Yeah, we know that," Ollie said.

"He also said 621 and 625 were occupied. We know 625 is Lucas Lauber's room. Who's in 621? It also has a connecting door, you know. I checked and it was closed. Even so—"

"Wait here!" Ollie hurried from the room. Less than a minute later he returned. "Scott Bell-James from Muscatine, Iowa, is what the registration says." He walked around the room and then said, "Sounds like a dead end to me."

"Are you sure?" I asked. "The name doesn't mean anything to me, but from the way Craig talked, I felt it meant more than just somebody taking the room by chance."

"I think you're right," Burton said. "Almost the clerk's first words to me were, 'Everybody wants room 623.'"

"Right!" I said. "When Deedra Knight asked for room 623, Craig insisted that everyone wanted that room and went on to say that 621 and 625 were taken—"

"As if they chose those rooms because they couldn't get 623," Burton said.

"Maybe we need to locate Scott Bell-James," Ollie said.

I wondered what took him so long to figure that out.

7

Ollie Viktor asked us to leave the tracking down of Scott Bell-James to him. He reminded me—not too sweetly—that he was the professional detective and we were in this only because he allowed us to participate. "And as long as you have something of value to add, you can stay."

He didn't add a threat, but the tone of his voice made his meaning clear. He left us and said he'd be back within half an hour.

That left Burton and me alone.

"I suppose you can start your retreat now," I said without enthusiasm.

He laughed and shook his head. "Now? And not stay involved in this? Don't you know me better than that? Besides, this might be a good diversion for me."

"Diversion? I thought you wanted rest."

"Change. Time away is what I want—what I need."

"I don't know much about how you preacher types work, but I assume you holy Joes have immense theological problems to grapple with so you can make thunderous pronouncements from the pulpit."

"You really love to play the ding-a-ling, don't you?"

"Do I? Do I really?" It was my best Southern accent and my most innocent look.

"Enough of that." He took my arm and said, "Let's go back into the garden area. Ollie will figure out where we are. You don't object, do you?"

Why would I object to walking with Burton?

As we walked out of the room, Ollie stood near the desk. He talked on his cell, but Craig hovered and didn't miss a word. Burton signaled that we were going out to the benches again and that we would turn right instead of left as before. Ollie waved us on.

We walked slowly down the path. By then, of course, he had released my arm, and I couldn't think of any way to get him to take it or to hold my hand. We found a small alcove with two benches that faced each other. On three sides of us grew an assortment of daylilies—some bright yellow, a few tiger lilies, and a variety of tall pristine white. Around the flowers the gardeners had planted sage and mint. I closed my eyes. Instead of being overpowering, the fragrance was just enough to enjoy.

This time we both sat on the same bench, and Burton leaned forward. "I want to tell you something."

I started to make a crack about liking to have him tell me anything, but the seriousness in those deep blue eyes told me to keep my mouth shut.

"You're the reason I'm here," he said.

"Me? You found out I was coming here?" I knew that wasn't what he meant, but I wanted to hear him say what he really meant. I liked the way this conversation had started.

"No, that's not what I meant." He turned away from me and played with his watchband for several seconds. "It's more than that. I'm in a dilemma. . .a real dilemma. I felt I had to get away for a few days to think." His voice became softer and lower so that I had to strain to hear the last few words. "It's you I need to think about."

"Me?" I asked. I loved hearing that but decided to play naive. "Why would you need to think about me?"

"You know I like you," he said.

"And I like you."

"A lot. I like you a lot."

"And I like you a lot, too."

"There you go with that ding-a-ling thing again," he said. But the hint of a smile made me know he liked it when I did that. He turned his face toward me. "I have feelings. . .strong feelings toward you, but—"

"But I'm a fallen woman, and you're the pure gentleman—"

"Don't, Julie."

"Don't what?"

"No game playing, at least not for a few minutes. Please," he said. "You know what I mean."

"Yes, I do." And of course I did. "I had no idea— really—that you felt, you know, that you liked—"

"It's this way. God is truly the most important thing in my life. He comes first. I—I, well, you're not a Christian, and—"

"Okay, I'll help you with this one," I said. When we met at the coast, I had told him about living with my religious-but-legalistic uncle. More than anyone else, my uncle Rich had turned me against the church, preachers, and Christianity. Burton had started to rebuild some of that destructive mind-set. I visited his church several times, and to my immense surprise, I liked the people. They were friendly, and I enjoyed the warm atmosphere. I had never felt that before inside a church building. Best of all, no one cornered me or tried to get me to rush down to the front and cry out for salvation.

"You mean you understand what I'm trying to say?" Burton asked.

I held up my hand. "My uncle had a saying. Okay, he had a lot of sayings, and most of them were aimed at me and my waywardness. One time a certain young preacher visited him and I liked him. Tall, blond. You know, a real hunk. And best of all, he wasn't married. He and I hit it off rather well, and I flirted with him."

Burton cocked his right eyebrow as if to ask, "Where is this story going?"

"After the man left, my uncle told me how shameless I had acted. He was correct, of course. I wouldn't have used the word *shameless*, but I knew what he meant. He raised his right hand. He always did that when he was getting ready to preach for my benefit."

Yes, it was one of those memories that sticks inside the brain and never seems to diminish.

~

Uncle Rich stood in the middle of the room. Usually his voice started low, and as he warmed up, it rose in pitch and volume. This time he started on a high octave, and anyone in the house could have heard him. "You're shameless. You're a hussy. You're a tempter sent from the devil himself."

I had heard Uncle Rich so many times that his preaching had begun to wear thin, and I had become immune to his insinuations. He had the amazing ability to read the vilest intention into everything I did. I wasn't quite ready to leave his house—that came about six weeks later—but I was tired of all his accusations.

"And what did I do this time?" I sighed loudly, but I knew that gesture was lost on my uncle.

"You have to ask? You flaunted yourself! You think I didn't see you lean toward him? You touched his hand! When you came back with the iced tea, you sat so close to him that I couldn't have put a piece of paper between you!" He raved on for at least a full minute.

"Really? You were watching me and all the sinful things I was doing? I thought you were listening to his talk about sanctification and the need for people to turn from idols of iniquity." I smiled at my uncle. "You see? I listened."

"How dare you mock me! You—you Jezebel! You temptress! You seductress! You wanton woman!"

"My, my, Uncle Rich, you must think about sex and sin a lot." I had overstepped that time. His face filled with anger, and I wondered if he was going to hit me.

"Let me warn you, young lady. You may end up corrupting that innocent man, but—"

"Corrupt? We had iced tea together in your presence. What kind of mind do you have?"

"He invited you to church, didn't he?"

"Yes, he did. And he said they had three hundred members."

"It's a beginning. I know how women like you work. You'll go to church and you'll play up to him and then trap him like a spider traps a fly."

"Can you really see all of that in my future?" I laughed. "I like him. Yeah, I like him a lot."

Uncle Rich came up to me and stopped only inches from my face. He stared into my eyes and said,

"If a man marries the devil's daughter, he'll certainly have trouble with his father-in-law."

"That's a good one! Probably the best one-liner you've ever come up with!"

I actually laughed. He must have heard that line somewhere, because Uncle Rich wasn't clever enough to think of anything original.

He slapped me.

I stared at him in surprise. It was the first time he had struck me. Several times in the past I had expected it, but he'd restrained himself.

"I hate you," I said calmly. "I hate you, and I detest your religion and despise your god and everything else you talk about."

"That's because you are of your father the devil."

"Okay, that's fine. So it's a family issue. I'm the devil's child and you're my uncle."

He slapped me again.

I ran from the room. That's when I determined I had to get away from there. I was still a college student and had no place to go. But I knew I had to find a place—any place. If he struck me and I put up with that, where would the abuse lead?

Two weeks later I met Dana Macie, had a quickie romance, married him, and a few weeks after our wedding, I learned he was into drugs. Later Dana died in a car accident.

As my mind came back to the present, I knew exactly what Burton struggled over. "If you marry the devil's daughter, you'll have problems with your father-in-law," I said. "Isn't that what you mean?"

Burton winced. "That's a bit strong."

"But the principle is right, isn't it?"

"Yes," he said softly. "Yes, I suppose—"

"So you came here to the inn because—"

"Because I had to figure out what to do. I care about you—I care a lot—a lot more than I ever thought I would—"

"So that's bad, is it?"

I'm not sure he heard my smart reply. "Julie, Julie, I've tried to hold back, but my feelings for you. . .well, I've never felt this strongly about a woman. Any woman. Ever."

"And the problem is?"

"Don't do that," he said. "You know the issue."

"You're right," I said. "I'll also tell you that I like you a lot, more than I ever thought possible. I don't know if I love you. I'm afraid to think about loving anyone." I was lying when I said those words, because I knew I did. "You know, one time down the chute with Dana Macie—"

"I remember your telling me."

"But it's more than your feelings, isn't it?" I asked. "Okay, I'll make it easier for you. According to your religion, we have no common foundation. You're committed to—to your God, and I'm a—"

"Yes, but you make it sound petty—"

"It is petty—and cruel—to me," I said, "but I also know it's absolutely serious to you."

"I could never marry a non-Christian."

"My uncle Rich was right about one thing. You're

a son of God, and I'm a daughter of the devil."

"Now you've gone from sounding petty to harsh."

"Maybe that's my protective barrier you've just crashed into. I don't want to be hurt. Not again."

"I wouldn't want to hurt you, Julie. Not ever," he said softly. "I hope you believe me."

"I know that."

"It doesn't have to be like this—"

"You mean if I turn to Jesus and—"

He stared at me, and I knew he wanted to take my hands, but I couldn't let him. I stood up. I wasn't ready to hear a long lecture on what I needed to do to get my life right with God. "I don't believe—at least not like you do, Burton. I'd like to believe. I'm open, or at least I try to be."

"What's the problem?"

"I suppose it's mostly my uncle Rich. His and other voices like his still lurk inside my head. Until I met you, I thought Christianity was for old people and idiots."

"And now?"

"It's not just for the old," I said. "No, I'm sorry. There I go. I'm at my worst when I'm tense or have to talk about my feelings."

"I know," he said. "You're good at picking up others' feelings, but not so clear about your own."

I sat on the bench across from him because I didn't trust myself. As I looked at James Burton, I knew—for the first time with absolute certainty—that I truly loved him. I also knew I didn't want to mess up his life. I'm too honest a person to say I believe in God unless I mean it.

"That's why I came here," he said. "I've missed you. I've wanted to call you half a dozen times every day, but I couldn't, and I won't. I had to get away and pray and ask God to help me."

"How did you ask? How did you pray?"

He hung his head, and light reflected on those gorgeous curls. "I prayed for God to—to give me a sign. If I was to hang on or if I was to totally avoid you. I had become desperate. I couldn't hear anything from God. I felt if I got away—"

"Away from any contact with me?"

He lifted his head and smiled. "Something like that."

"So we're both here at the Cartledge Inn and neither of us knew the other would be here. Do you think God arranged that, or was it a trick of the devil? Uncle Rich would say the latter."

"I prefer to think more about God than I do the devil."

Our eyes met. I didn't know what to say or do. Obviously he didn't either. So we stared.

I love this man, I said to myself. *I do. But I can't—I can't go his way.*

8

A lovers' quarrel?" Ollie asked.
I hadn't heard him approach and wasn't aware of his presence until he spoke. Despite his being a large man, he walked quietly. I wondered if that had been part of his police training.

"Hardly," I said. I was glad he had come, because Burton and I didn't know what to say to each other. I wanted to kiss him and he wanted to run away, but neither of us had moved.

"Did you learn anything about room 621?" Burton asked.

"I still don't know anything about Scott Bell-James, but he did write down his cell number when he checked in. I left him a voice message and asked him to call me."

"Thanks, Ollie, for letting us be part of this," I said. "I know we're amateurs—"

"And you are," he said without rancor in his voice. "But I'm open to any kind of help."

"I wanted to ask you something," I said. "It's about Deedra Knight. Why would someone kill her? I assume she wanted the diamonds. At least it makes sense that she was looking for them. But why murder her? If she found the diamonds, wouldn't it be easier to take them from her?"

"Probably," he said.

"But why kill her?" I persisted. "Unless, of course, she found them and the murderer could only take them from her by shooting her. Seems drastic."

"Or maybe the killer didn't want anyone alive to identify him," Burton said. "Or her."

"A strong possibility," Ollie said.

Burton looked at Ollie. "But until you know that's the reason, what do you plan to do? What's your next step?"

Ollie sat next to his former classmate. "I plan to talk to anyone who can shed any light on this situation." His voice was calm and pleasant. As a professional, I wondered how his moods could shift so easily. I wondered if this erratic behavior was typical or if this case was causing a big emotional strain.

Ollie talked for a while, but I didn't hear him. I was absorbed in watching him. His hand had shaken slightly before, but now it was steady. He smiled the way he had when we first met. Something was different about him, and in the back of my head, something clicked. I had worked with clients like him before, but I couldn't pull the information into my conscious mind.

"Good idea," Burton said, and I snapped back to attention.

"Jason Omore will be here in a minute," Ollie said. "I called his room and asked him to join us. I told him we'd be out here." He smiled at me. "After we learn everything he knows, perhaps you'll open up and tell me the rest of what you know about Lauber." He leaned forward, about a foot from my face. His green eyes narrowed as if he were trying to see inside my head. "And I know you're still holding back."

Before I could reply, Jason Omore came into view.

He had picked a yellow rose and held it out to me. "I don't have permission to do this from the owners," he said, "but I do not think they will mind if I pluck one rose to give to such a beautiful woman. Does not beauty attract beauty?"

"I like you better all the time," I said. I took the flower and held it to my nose and inhaled the scent. So many of the roses these days have little fragrance, but this was different. The pungent aroma filled my nostrils.

Jason sat next to me and faced the detective. "You wish to ask more questions, is that so?" Before he looked at Ollie, he glanced at me, and I think he winked, but it was so quick I wasn't positive.

"Tell us more about you and Lauber at the prison."

"Is there much to tell? I do not know, but I shall try." Jason held his hand to his face. "Even the odor of the rose remains. Do you say odor? Is that not a negative word?"

"Try fragrance," Burton said. I could tell from his expression that he knew Jason was creating a diversion on purpose.

"As you know, I am a Christian," Jason Omore said. "I am also a student sent here by my government so that I may return and develop—"

"Yeah, yeah," Ollie said. "You can skip that part. Get to Lauber."

"Yes, but of course, I shall do that. At the prison in Rome, I spoke with many of the inmates. As you may know, in prisons and jails, many volunteer groups come regularly to present worship services and Bible studies. I chose to talk to them individually. Because I was a doctoral student from Emory University, I had no problems in moving freely around the prison."

"And how did you meet Stefan?" I asked.

"First, as you may know, he was at two different prisons before they transferred him to Rome—"

"Yeah, I know how the system works," Ollie said. "With good conduct come better conditions." He cleared his throat and added, "So answer the question."

"I had posted the information at various places in the prison that I wished to study individual inmates and their behavior. All things were confidential. More than sixty of them showed up."

"That's a lot," I said.

He laughed, and his whole face participated in the exercise. I had rarely seen a person so happy. I wondered what made him so joyful. It was more than his face; something about the way he behaved exuded a kind of aura of peace and quiet joy. The more I was around Jason Omore, the more I liked him.

"That is easy to explain, is it not? Some thought it would help them make early parole. I had to assure them that their participation would not make a difference. For others, they came to the meeting out of boredom. Some left the facilities during the day for work details, but the others had nothing much to claim their attention."

"And Stefan was among which group?" Ollie asked.

"He worked on detail, is the way I think it is said. He often worked for ten hours each day. It was volunteer work, but he seemed always the first to volunteer for any task."

"Did you wonder why?" Ollie asked.

"But of course, and I asked."

"And what did he say?"

"I had seen Mr. Lauber before, of course. He was different from most of the others."

"You didn't answer my question," Ollie said, "but maybe you'll answer this. In what way was he different?"

"Many of the inmates had marked themselves—tattoos, many tattoos. Others carried scars from fights. Too often I saw old faces, hard faces on young men. He was in age maybe, I don't know—"

"Thirty-seven," Ollie said. "According to our records, he would have been thirty-eight in November."

"Yes, but it was more. He shaved and dressed as if he had a purpose each day. How can I say it? Most of them seemed to have nothing. Something else also. He read. He read many, many books, did he not?"

"What kind of books?" Ollie asked.

"Everything. The prison had no real library, even though I tried to get them to start one. A few books were in the recreation room, and there is a room where they may enter and read, but little of intellectual stimulation. People cannot send books to individuals, but only publishing houses can do so. So he received many such books that way by ordering them from the publishers. Once he read them, he left them in the reading room for others."

"How did he pay for them?"

"I did not ask, but one day he said his brother gave him money."

The three of us looked away from Jason and at each other. Our silent faces asked how that could be. They supposedly hated each other.

"Do you know anything about his brother?" Burton asked.

"Of that I know little. I met him but one time in the prison. He came to visit. By then, Stefan was truly my friend, and he introduced him to me. We did not exchange words. He seemed to be in great haste to leave."

"That was the only time you saw him?"

"Yes, of course, except for yesterday."

"What?" Ollie jumped up and grabbed Jason's T-shirt as if he wanted to strangle the African. "What are you holding back?"

Jason said nothing, but his eyes met Ollie's and he did not flinch. Ollie finally released him and moved back.

"You did not ask if I had seen him here. It was a surprise to me to see him, of course."

"When did you see him? Where? Here in the hotel?"

"I saw him but yesterday. I did not look at the time, but I know it was before 6:30. Perhaps ten minutes, but I do not know."

"How do you know the time?"

"Because my doctoral adviser promised to call me at 6:30." He held up his cell phone. "I wanted to get out of my room, and I was moving toward the front entrance of the building. I wanted to walk away from the inn and toward the expressway. I do not have a motor vehicle, and I wanted to see a different landscape.

That is when we met."

"And exactly where did you meet Lucas?" Ollie asked.

"When he exited from the elevator, is that not so?"

"Did he acknowledge you?" Burton asked.

"At first not. I think he recognized me, but he would have walked past as if he must be in a large hurry. He walked quite rapidly. Perhaps he did not remember my name, but—"

"Did you speak to him?" I asked.

"Would it not have been rude for me not to do so?"

Ollie took a long, deep sigh and said, "Please, Jason, just tell us. Don't make me pull out every tiny fragment of information."

"Yes, that I can do." Jason momentarily closed his eyes. "He wore a blazer that was of the color gray, a light gray. His trousers were of a darker shade of the color gray. And as I said, he walked very fast, as if in a large hurry." He turned to me. "Large hurry? Is that correct English? I think it is not correct?"

"We understand what you mean," Ollie said. "Just move on."

"I greeted him and extended my hand," Jason said. "I introduced myself, and he said he did remember me. We both were going in the same direction, so I walked out of the inn with him and to his car. He drove away. That is all."

"That's all?" Ollie asked. His anger was almost at the exploding point. "What did you talk about as you walked to his car? What kind of car was it? Did he say where he was going? Did he explain why he had been at the hotel?"

"Oh, is that what you wish to know?" Jason said. "He told me that he had been to see his brother, but he was not in his room. I had seen Stefan perhaps an hour earlier when he stopped at my room."

"Why your room?" I asked.

"To give me a Bible and—"

"Okay, and then Stefan left you? Is that correct?" Ollie asked.

I wondered how Ollie solved any crimes if he was always so uptight and explosive.

"Lucas said he had come because Stefan needed to sign a paper, and he was late for a place he had to be for a meeting, and he regretted that he could no longer wait for his brother."

"Just that?" the detective asked.

"I said I would drop by his room later and ask him to call, but Lucas said I should not bother. That was all."

"Nothing else."

"My cell phone rang then. It was exactly 6:30. My adviser is punctually absolute." He laughed. "Sorry, absolutely punctual. English is so difficult, is it not, especially with where to place the adjectives, is that not so?"

"And he drove away?"

"Yes, and it was a green vehicle. A Mercedes, but the year of the vehicle I do not know," Jason said. "But it was not a vintage model—not—not old, I mean."

Ollie waved at him to stop explaining.

"Was there anything unusual about him? Anything that struck you as strange or unusual?" I asked.

"But one thing only. It was a paper he held in his

hand. I could not read it, but it was, how do you say it? Crumpled? No, it was also that, but—"

"Torn?" I asked.

"Yes!" His eyes lit up. "Sometimes I forget English words. It was torn—no, ripped. Fragmented. Yes, that is the word. It was but almost all of one page, and does that not make it a fragment?" Without waiting for an answer, he said, "I noticed it because the fragment was not straight at the bottom. You know, if I take a sheet of paper from a tablet, both top and bottom are even—"

"Okay, okay, I got it," Ollie said. "Torn. Ripped. Shredded. Fragmented. Whatever. Could you read it?"

He shook his head. "And would it not have been rude to try to do so?"

"Did your people find the remaining portion of the paper?" I asked.

Ollie shook his head. "Not that I know. It certainly wasn't among the evidence collected."

"It would have been such a small portion," Jason added. "But a pinch—I think is how you say it."

Ollie waved him away.

"I have a couple of questions I want to ask," Burton said. "Would you tell us about your time together in prison? What happened?"

"Yes, that I can do. I did not like Stefan at first because he said rude things—perhaps rude is not the word. Vulgar? Yes, he spoke with vulgar—with vulgarity—about my faith and about God."

"Tell us, will you?" I asked.

"Let's go back to the room," Ollie said. "This is a little too public."

We followed him back to the meeting room.

9

This is the story Jason Omore told us:

I had noticed Stefan because he was different, and that I have already said. He told me the first time in the meeting that he didn't want to hear me talk about God.

"Then you must close your ears or walk away," I said to him. "God is not something I can push aside because you are afraid to hear of Him."

"Afraid? What makes you think I'm afraid?" His voice was very low, what you call a bass.

"Are you not afraid?" I asked.

"I just don't want to hear anything about religion," he said. "I had a couple of injections when I was a boy and now I'm inoculated. I don't need another dose."

"That I can understand for your sake," I said, "but for my sake, if I cannot speak about God, it is as if I would be forced to walk with only one leg." I turned from him and spoke to the others in the room. I did that to enable him to get up and leave if he chose to do so. I did not wish to embarrass anyone. By then we had only fourteen men left in the room. "Each of you has volunteered to come here. If you choose to remain with my program, I will record the information, but your names will never appear. I must do this to defend my work at the university." I looked around. "There are liars and crooked people in this place, you know."

Most of them laughed, and several hooted and clapped.

"No one will hear your voice—unless it is because my supervisor wishes to up-check."

"Check up, you mean!" one of them called out and many laughed. I made that error on purpose, of course. From their responses I knew they wanted to trust me.

They had a few questions, but most of all, they simply wished to talk, and I waited patiently for them to speak. I explained that I studied quite diligently to understand behavior in humans. "It may surprise you, of course, but we truly have criminal activity in Kenya. We wish to understand behavior of every kind."

They truly loved it when I spoke like that. They thought I was extremely naive, and I did not mind that they thought so.

After that I looked around, and Stefan Lauber had not left. I was surprised, but I made no mention of his presence still with us.

In the middle of my first session with the group, one of the men stood up. "Why would you come here? You're not like some of those who want notches on their guns to record each of the converts they've shot out of hell and landed in heaven."

This time Stefan clapped loud and long. It was the first time he had responded as a member of the group.

Did I not laugh at that? Yes, indeed, I did laugh. Then I explained that I had once been a very bad person in my native Kenya. I had used *pombe*—native beer—every night without fail. I beat my wife if she argued with me, and I stole cattle from other farmers. But one day God changed my life.

I told them about a man named Erasto Otieno who had come to our village and told me that God loved me and God's Spirit would never give me peace until I surrendered. He also said he would not leave our village until I believed in Jesus.

"Is this not strange?" I asked the men.

I must explain our African custom to you. That man, Erasto, stayed in our village for five days. In our culture, a guest stays until the host tells him to go. That is the way it is, although Western culture is changing our ways, those of us who live far from the cities still honor the ways of our ancient parents.

I explained to the inmates that I could not ask Erasto to leave because my wife wanted to hear him speak and so did my parents. My two sons begged me to let him say his many words. Unlike your culture, I could have not walked away from him. He was my guest. For me to do so would have been a serious insult.

So Erasto spoke to me, to each of us, and he seemed never to be without an excuse to preach about Jesus. I would offer him a drink of water, and he would tell me that Jesus was living water. We had just gotten electricity in our area, and when I turned on the lights, he would say that Jesus was the light of the world.

Yes, he irritated me, but he also did it with love in his voice, and something made me listen to his words. I could not have walked away—that would have been a rude thing. I seemed to have no choice but to listen. He was not there to get me to join some *dini*—some religious group—and I believe he came as a man of love for other human beings.

Before the end of the fifth day, I believed. I believed

because of the words he spoke, but I also believed because of the way he spoke the words. In his face I saw that he would die for Jesus if asked to do so.

I confessed my sins and promised to follow Jesus. I was weak, and I stumbled many times, but I kept on. One day, perhaps a year later, I learned that Erasto had died. A witch doctor in the primitive area of Kadem Location had poisoned his food. When I heard that, I knew—deep inside my heart—I knew that I must carry on Erasto's work. I would not be a preacher as he was, but I could become useful to God in whatever field I chose.

After I answered that call, did I not witness openness in many hearts?

But about the men: After I answered their questions, they had nothing more to ask. I waited and I knew they trusted me, so I gave them forms to fill out. They were simple questions and asked only for basic information about themselves, their crimes, and how they felt about what they had done in breaking laws. I was careful not to ask if they were guilty.

When everyone had completed the papers, I said, "If any of you wish to stay and talk about Jesus, I shall be most pleased to do that."

After I dismissed them, eleven men stayed. They sat at heavy wooden tables and on hard chairs. One of those who did not leave was Stefan Lauber.

I spoke to them. The others had all been to church, had all thought they were members of the kingdom of God at one time, but they also committed crimes. None of them were murderers. Not those in that prison. Most of them were there on drug charges, theft of vehicles, and other nonviolent crimes. Two of them had been in prison before, but the rest were there for the first time—and I hope the only time.

As I have said, Stefan Lauber was different from the others. He was the only one with a college education, and there was another factor about him. Dare I use the English word mystical? It was as if God had chosen me and sent me to the prison to give him the information for which he had been waiting many years. He did not know he was waiting, but had not God put a deep longing into his heart? Later he would tell me these words: "I felt as if I have waited all my life to meet you."

I provided him with books to read—as many as three a week. One of my professors was kind enough to pay for them and have a publisher send them. Stefan read the books—every one of them. One day I saw him reading the Bible, but he did not understand much of what he read, so I helped him, did I not? From then on, he spent at least one hour each day in reading the Bible, mostly the New Testament. He would stay with a chapter or a portion until he could say to me, "Yes, I understand."

Four days before his early release, Stefan asked to see me. The guard normally escorted inmates from place to place, but they did not do that with Stefan. Yes, a guard was present, but he walked beside him, as if they were two friends. Like Paul the apostle of old, he had won the respect of those who were his captors.

He came into the room, and the guard stepped outside. As soon as the door closed, Stefan fell on his knees in front of my desk. "Please, please help me."

The agony written across his face showed such severe

pain, I went around to him, pulled him up, and embraced him. I said nothing and waited for him to speak.

"I have been a terrible sinner," Stefan said. "And I know I must change."

"Yes, that is good," I said. "We must all change."

"But it's more than that. I have stolen from people."

"Can you not return what you have taken?"

"That's the problem. I want to follow Jesus, but I want to keep what I've stolen because I'll end up back in prison if I attempt to return the stolen items." He laughed at himself. "That sounds terrible, but it's true."

I embraced him tightly—I had been doing that for some weeks. He embraced me just as tightly. Before I released him, I prayed that the Holy Spirit would make him want to return what he had stolen. Just that much.

As I started to walk away, he said, "You are the most happy man I have ever known. Why is that?"

"Is that not what my name says?" I answered.

Most strangely he stared at me and said, "I don't understand."

"My name. My African name. It is Omore. In my language, which is called Luo, the word means a happy person or one who reflects happiness."

"Yes, you are a credit to your name," he said.

The words came with such softness, tears leaped from my eyes. I am a happy person, that is true, but I am far from the kind of person I wish to be. Instead of answering, I could speak only a word of thanks.

He opened the door and started out, stopped, and

turned. "Omore, my happy friend, you are the kind of Christian I would like to become."

Those words touched me deeply, and once again the tears leaped from my eyes.

The next day I had to return to Emory University for research and to meet with two of my professors. When I returned, I learned that Stefan had been released. I thought that was the end of our relationship.

To my surprise, three days later I received an e-mail from him; he invited me to come here to the Cartledge Inn and to study. He informed me that he had sufficient funds to pay all my expenses and that they were not stolen funds. Was I not most pleased to accept such an offer?

When I came to Cartledge Inn, he met me and greeted me before he introduced me to the members of the staff. We were together every morning for at least an hour at a time. Some days it was for longer.

———

Jason wiped tears from his eyes. "He was my friend. My good friend. Never have I had a friend I have loved so much as Stefan Lauber. He planned to return to Kenya with me to meet my wife and my children. But now that cannot be."

I thought he was through, but he said, "It is now my intention that my next son will be named Stefano in his honor. Among my people it is the highest honor we can give another—the greatest honor I can offer in his memory—to name my child after him."

"Very touching," Ollie said. "Very."

"And you have no idea how Stefan resolved the problem?" Burton asked.

Jason shook his head. "No, I do not *know*. I cannot say such a word; however, I believe that he did the right thing, whatever that was. That is how my *rafiki*—my friend—behaved. He had many, many struggles inside his heart, but in the end he always did the right thing."

I glanced at Ollie and asked, "Do you suppose that's why he was killed? To prevent his returning the diamonds?"

"I can think of another reason," he said.

"Which is?" I asked.

"Someone else wanted the diamonds and Lauber refused to give them up. He wanted to hold on to them himself."

"Makes sense as another possibility," I said, but I didn't believe my own words. I sensed Jason had been right about Lauber.

"But what did he do with the diamonds?" Burton asked.

10

E xcuse me." Craig opened the door without knocking. "Your new room is ready for you, Mr. Oliver." He was quiet and quite professional. He smiled at me—and he almost pulled off that friendly-but-plastic smile many professionals develop. Maybe if he worked at it, he would learn to fake it well. I liked him better in flustered mode.

What Jason told us of his experiences with Stefan presented me with a different picture of the man than what I'd heard from anyone else. He must have been a good man—or maybe he had *become* a good man.

As if he had read my mind, Burton said, "God can change people. That's the divine specialty, you know."

"So they tell me." That smart answer came out before I realized what I had said. I opened my mouth to apologize, but Burton smiled as if to say, "Apology not needed."

He knows me well—maybe too well.

Ollie thanked Craig and turned to Jason. "You can leave. I'll call you if I need anything else."

I thought Ollie's tone was a bit dismissive, but I said nothing. Burton shook Jason's hand as if to make up for Ollie's harsh treatment.

"You are also a good man," Jason said, "for I can see it in your eyes. Yes, you are truly a very good man."

Burton turned his head away, but I think he blushed.

Ollie had already dismissed Jason and said to Burton

and me, "I've arranged for a suite where we can talk and meet with anyone who has anything to tell us." Without waiting for a reply, he led the way.

I patted Jason Omore's shoulder and said, "Thanks. That helps me understand a few things." I wanted to talk to him, perhaps alone, and I hoped I'd have the opportunity. Like Burton, this man exuded a vital connection to God. This was so unusual. Other than Burton, I had met only one man who had exuded any kind of vital, warm relationship to God. A man named Simon Presswood whom I'd met at Palm Island. So here I was again with two men, both of whom lived a vital relationship with God.

Has God decided to gang up on me? I didn't want to answer my own question; it might be true.

Instead of going to the elevators, Ollie led us past them. We made a left turn and went directly to room 127, a suite with a large sitting room and a bedroom, although the bedroom door was closed. For my tastes, the room was far too austere with an overabundance of pale colors, pale fabrics, pale woods, and delicate paintings. The room needed vibrant colors, rich fabrics, and exciting new paintings. But then I don't suppose guests rented the suite to admire the room. Aside from the usual desk and several floor lamps, the room held two large sofas, both of a boring ocher color, and a wing chair of equally drab yellow.

"Sit down," Ollie said in a commanding voice. "In order to make us comfortable, the owners of the Cartledge Inn promised to send in refreshments this afternoon."

I attempted a smile as I watched Ollie's hand

tremble slightly. Earlier the harsh tone was there along with the tremor. Was it Parkinson's? Surely he wasn't on some kind of drugs, was he? Although I didn't like him much, I could hardly think he'd be into something like that. So why did his hand tremble at times?

I checked my watch. It was nearly 2:30. I could hardly believe the time had passed so quickly. Burton and I had not eaten lunch, but I didn't mind. That might give me a good excuse to snag Burton for a long, quiet dinner.

Not that we had gotten far in solving the murder, but I had spent a few minutes alone with Burton. I knew how he felt about me, and his confession had surprised me. Until then I thought the attraction was only a one-sided romantic infatuation. When we met at Palm Island, he had playfully said he liked me a lot, but he'd also told me then about his unwillingness to get involved with someone who was of a different faith. I laughed to myself after I thought about those words. No, it wasn't a different faith. Mine was simply no faith, but he had tried to be gentle and sweet and wouldn't have said anything to hurt my feelings.

For several minutes I seriously considered an attempt to fake the faith, but I knew I couldn't do that. If anything ever worked out between us—and that meant I'd have to become a Christian first—it would definitely have to be real. I had given serious thought at one time to becoming a true vamp as my uncle Rich said I was, and had a few nice daydreams about saving Burton from all the bondage of religion. But I knew he was too determined, and even if I had succeeded, he wouldn't have been happy.

So if there was to be a change, I had to be the one to make it. But I didn't want to change. I didn't want to become one of those holy-holy types. Why did I need to have some kind of religious experience or change? I was a good person—not perfect, but I was an ethical person. But why did Burton have to be such a kind, sweet person? Why did he have to be so accepting of others?

A uniformed waiter came into the room with cold water, juice, and Cokes. He had hardly gone when someone knocked.

"Come in!" Ollie yelled.

A muscular African American man, about five feet five, walked into the room. More accurately, he swaggered into the room. Stocky, with a big chest and bigger arms, he had a neck as thick as a wharf post. He looked as if he snapped railroad ties in half for exercise or fun.

His dark brown eyes were far lighter than his skin, and his bushy black beard was lightly salted with curly white hairs. That touch of frosting was the only thing about him, other than the whites of his eyes, that was not very, very dark. I guessed his age to be early forties. Probably to emphasize his dark features, he wore black slacks and a black shirt. I might have been afraid of him if I had met him on the street, except for one thing: The brightness of those dark brown eyes twinkled in a way that would have pushed aside any trepidation.

To me he seemed such a strange contrast—except for those eyes, he looked like a man ready to confront anyone who stood in his way. Or as my administrative assistant would say, "That dude shows plenty of 'tude."

"You left a message on my business phone. Said you wanted to see me." He looked directly at Oliver Viktor. "I'm here. What do you want?" As he stared at Ollie, his eyes lost that softness.

"Well, well, so we meet again after such a long time," Ollie said. "Hey, Burton and Glamour Girl, this is Nicky Harrison. On the street they call him Chips."

"They call me Chops. C-h-o-p-s," he said, "but you knew that."

"Yeah, that's right," Ollie said. "I'd forgotten." But it was obvious he hadn't forgotten. I wondered why he wanted to antagonize the man.

The stranger stared at me, looked me over carefully, and said, "Mr. Smart-Mouth here think he so funny, but don't know nothin' about crackin' jokes. Yeah, they still call me Chops."

"That's an unusual name," I said because I didn't know how else to respond.

"That's 'cause I usta be a tough guy. If anyone messed with me or my boys from the hood, I chopped him good with my fists."

"Do you still chop?" Burton asked.

"Not since the Lord Jesus chopped me down to size. No, sir."

"Yeah, that's right," Ollie said, "I heard you got religion in prison."

"Not *religion*, Mr. Policeman; you done heard wrong," Chops said. "I was sentenced to ninety-five years in the federal prison for murder and four cases of rape."

"Yeah, I remember."

"You should!" Those eyes, so soft minutes ago, blazed in anger.

"I'm surprised you're out and able to breathe real air like the rest of us."

"No, you ain't. You knew."

"Guess I did," Ollie said.

"And it prob'bly ruined your already miserable day." Before Ollie could make another wisecrack, Chops said, "The man with the big, scary badge is right. I was in prison, but I was innocent. And to be honest about everything, I did a lot of bad things—never murder or rape—but plenty of bad things, and I got away with them all. But in prison I prayed and—"

"Oh, here it comes," Ollie said. "Sorry I brought it up—"

"Listen, Mr. Policeman, you let me set the record straight. I started to pray in prison—right in the federal pen here in Atlanta. I promised God that if He'd set me free, I'd serve Him forever." He stopped and smiled. His face changed when he smiled, as if all the 'tude had vanished. "And that's what happened. The government began to introduce all that DNA stuff, don't you know? And they proved I couldn't have done any of those crimes. Not any of them! And now I've gotten an official apology, have a pending case against the police department—your police department and your former partner. I've been out in the big world. I'm free from prison and free from sin. Best of all, I've been born again for five years."

"Yeah, so I heard." Ollie made no attempt to hide the sneer in his voice.

"And so you still hate me, don't you?" Chops said. "But I'd like to tell you something." He stepped up close to Ollie, who was several inches taller, but Chops didn't look intimidated. "You did your thing, and that was okay, 'cause while I was inside, God did His thing. After I got it figured out, just like with ol' Peter, the doors swung open for me, and I ain't never looked back no more. Been out a year."

"Yeah, well, that's, uh, very nice," Ollie said, and he didn't back away, "but that's not the reason I asked you to come."

Chops Harrison laid his beefy arm on Ollie's shoulder and then straightened his tie. "Yeah, you remember good. Real good. I don't like you, and God don't say I gotta do that, but I forgive you."

"Like I care a great deal," Ollie said. But the harshness of his voice seemed to have diminished. As I watched the exchange, I felt as if Chops had finally intimidated him.

The black man patted Ollie on the cheek. "Notice, I didn't give you no kiss of peace, but I ain't gonna put a hurtin' on you."

"Uh, so, uh, you and Ollie know—"

Chops interrupted me. "Know each other? How about that, Mr. Policeman?" He smiled at me, and the twinkle was back in his eyes. "Yeah, this dude don't only knowed me. He knowed me 'cause his partner it was that turned over all the so-called evidence. He knowed I was innocent."

Ollie shrugged. "What's the difference? It got you off the streets—"

"You are sure right about that, Mr. Policeman. Even if you allowed your partner to pump up the evidence." He stressed the last word so that all three syllables received the same inflection.

Ollie shrugged again dismissively. "You know how it is—"

"Oh, I know," Chops said, "and I ain't never expected an apology from you. And 'course, you ain't big enough to give me none neither."

"I was just trying to do my duty," Ollie said, "just trying to do my duty like I'm trying to do right now."

"And may I assist you to do your duty?" Chops asked. He gently pushed Ollie into the wing chair and sat on the sofa across from him. "As a public-minded citizen in good standing in this community, how may I render assistance to the police department?"

The change in his voice amazed me. He had come in sounding like some tough guy who bounded out of the Wide World of Wrestling or Atlanta's inner city. But this time his tough, uneducated street talk was gone.

"Okay, let's cut through all the garbage and get this straight," Ollie said. "I didn't like you before, and I don't like you now, despite the DNA—"

"You know, that's funny," Chops said. "I didn't like you before. Now I just feel sorry for you. You're such a small man on the inside. An extremely small man."

Ollie flushed, but to his credit, he didn't say anything.

Chops spotted the refreshments, hopped off the sofa, and went over to the ice-filled box. He took out a bottle of water. I half expected him to bite off the end. He slowly turned the cap, peeled it off, and took several sips of water. Even in taking the water, there was both a gentleness and a grace in his movement that seemed so different from the man who had walked into the room only ten minutes earlier.

"So you wanted me here to answer questions," Chops said. "As a law-abiding citizen in good standing with a clean police record, I have come at your request." He bowed from the waist. "How may I assist you?"

"You called room 623 eight times in the last five days," Ollie said.

"I don't know about eight times, but if you say so. After all, why would you lie to me? You represent the —"

"You deny you've called room 623?"

"No, I don't *deny* anything. I called Stefan Lauber. I didn't know what room he was in. When the receptionist answered, I asked her to connect me."

"Yeah, right," Ollie said. "Okay, let that go for now. Why did you call?"

"Why do you want to know?"

"Maybe I'm just a curious kind of guy." Ollie leaned forward, and anger filled his face.

"Stefan Lauber was murdered last night," Burton said. "Ollie Viktor is investigating the crime."

Chops paled when he heard the word *murdered*. He staggered backward and sat on the sofa next to me. "Stefan? Murdered?"

"You didn't know?"

He shook his head. Tears filled his eyes, but he said only, "Stefan? Stefan? But why?"

"Tell us about the phone calls," Ollie said. The anger had disappeared from his face and voice. I think he believed Chops.

"I can't believe. . . I just can't—"

"Sorry if I can't give you time to mourn," Ollie said, "but this is a murder investigation, and—"

"Stop it," I said to Ollie. "Can't you see the shock on his face? Even you can give him a minute to absorb this."

"Whatever," Ollie said, but I felt he heard me and was ashamed at his behavior.

For perhaps a full minute no one said anything. We just stared at Chops. If we hadn't been watching, I think he would have broken down and cried. I didn't know anything about the relationship between Stefan and Chops, but it was obvious the man cared for the late Stefan Lauber.

"He had planned to help me—help us—with a project in Decatur." Chops said the words so softly I strained to hear him.

"What kind of project?" Ollie asked.

"Does it matter to you? It was legitimate. That's all you need to know."

"Make it easy on yourself, Chops. Just tell me what I want to know."

Chops Harrison stared out the large window for several seconds as if debating whether to speak. He sighed and mumbled, "Okay."

"Okay, what?" Ollie said.

"I have nothing to hide. It's just so—so—" With his large right hand, Chops wiped both of his eyes before he turned his face toward the detective and said, "You see, I met Stefan when he was in prison up in Floyd County." He turned to me and smiled. "I was only a visitor. I came to see Too Tall Tom Tomlinson, one of my boys who had messed up. I thought he was clean, police caught him. Two *honest* policemen. Too Tall was slamming ice."

"He was injecting ice—the purest form of meth," I whispered to Burton. In the past year, I heard that term a lot at our center.

Burton nodded his thanks, because he obviously hadn't understood.

"Yeah, and it was a tough one and his second knockdown, but Too Tall Tomlinson is going to make it this time. He's now in rehab, voluntarily."

"Okay, so you were at Floyd County," Ollie said, "and that's where I lost the trail."

"So while I was there, I met a neat dude from Africa named Jason Omore. I can give you his cell number if—"

"Jason is here at the inn," I said.

"Really? I'll look him up. Great man of God. You know him, huh?"

"We do," Burton said. "And we like him."

"How could you diss him? Mr. Policeman, Omore and I, man, we started rappin' about things, you know, and we got pretty tight, and he introduced me to Stefan. We chilled for maybe ten minutes."

Chops had reverted to his street talk, and I wondered if he had done it to antagonize Ollie.

"How long ago was that?" Ollie asked.

"Don't know. Don't matter none now, do it?"

"Just answer," Ollie said. His voice sounded angry again.

As I listened to the two men, it seemed as if they both shifted from one style to another. Ollie's hand shook just a little more than it had before Chops entered the room.

Chops closed his eyes as if in thought and said

quietly, "Maybe a year ago. Yeah, just a year. After that I wrote Too Tall a letter every week."

"Yeah, right, of course," said Ollie. "You wrote—actually wrote—letters?"

"Excuse me," Chops said, "but I have earned a master's degree in journalism from the University of Georgia. That's what I do now. I'm a journalist. In case you don't know what that means, I'm the assistant bureau chief for the AP. Uh, sir, that's the Associated Press."

"Well, miracles happen, don't they?" Ollie said.

"Indeed, they do," Chops said. "And by the grace of God, I'm one of them."

"Okay, point well taken," Ollie said. "Tell me more about the project in Decatur to which Lauber was *purportedly* going to offer help."

"Oh, it was more than an offer," Chops said and genuinely smiled. The glint in his eyes had returned, and his voice softened. "We finalized plans to set up a series of homes there. It's a new concept in children's homes—what we used to call orphanages. Instead of one large, institutional setting, we have decided to set up group homes. They're clustered together, but we will have such group clusters in other parts of the country. He had already put up a grant for a similar cluster near Auburn, Alabama."

"Yeah, yeah, I got it," Ollie said. "Just tell us about the place in Decatur."

"Stefan bought eight houses. One is built and ready to move into. That was to be his house. The second is—"

"What's the address?" I asked.

"It's off Columbia Drive, and the street is called Royal Path Court."

"And is the house—the one already built—numbered 623?" I asked.

"Exactly. Yes, that's the one. Have you been there?"

"Okay, okay, I understand. I know everything I need to know, okay?" an extremely irritated Ollie said. "Can we just stay with basics?"

"First I don't tell you enough; now I tell you too much," Chops said. I saw the faintest hint of a smile. This man was bright and about ten yards ahead of the detective.

"And the phone calls?" I watched Ollie's face; he concealed all trace of emotion while Chops spoke. "Why did you call him?"

"All the calls had to do with minor problems and details about the program. We wanted to name the cluster after him, but he said no. I pushed him, but he refused. We finally decided to name it after Jason Omore." He turned to Burton and said, "His name—Omore—means a happy person. So we're calling the venture Happy Face Homes."

"And you can prove all this?" Ollie asked.

"You'll have to ask Jason. He told me that was the meaning of his name."

Ollie slammed his fist on the arm of the chair. "You know what I meant."

"Oh, that? Yes, I can prove it about as well as you can disprove it," Chops said. "I have all the paperwork, but I don't record telephone calls."

"Too bad the government will have to take it all

away," Ollie said. "Lauber used stolen money, you know."

"No, he didn't," Chops said. "That's what part of the phone calls were about, especially the last one."

"Okay, so tell me," Ollie said, and his voice was about as sneering as I had ever heard it. "And try talking loud, will you? If you shout, the argument becomes even more convincing."

I'm not normally an angry person, but I wanted to get up and slap Ollie's face about ten times. And if he still kept that smug look, I would volunteer for another ten times.

To my surprise, Chops didn't react. "You may or may not know that Stefan had been an investment broker. He started out totally legit and made a lot of big bucks doing that. Good money. In fact, extremely good money."

"Oh, but of course," Ollie said. "Another innocent in the world."

"I refer to the period prior to the diamond robbery. We can prove his honesty. I investigated him thoroughly before I became involved. For example, Stefan invested fifty-five thousand dollars in a start-up company close to thirty years ago—I think it was around 1977 or 1978, but I'd have to check my research. You see, another factor is that I wanted to write his biography. He refused but said maybe one day. So I collected information and—"

"Yeah, I got that," Ollie said. "About 1977 or 1978, what happened? I can hardly wait to hear this."

"Good, because it's a great story. Stefan invested in a start-up company owned by two guys named

Bernie Marcus and Arthur Blank. They called it the MB Associates—"

"Okay, so—"

"So they later changed the name to Home Depot. Maybe you've heard of them. That fifty-five grand has made so much money that maybe a year before the diamond robbery, he sold his share of the company, reinvested in Google.com, and—"

"Oh, I am so impressed."

"Ollie, cut it out, okay?" Burton said softly. "Let's just listen."

"Yes, I have all the paper trail, and furthermore, three months ago Stefan sold his Google stock—all legitimately owned—and put every penny into a nonprofit organization. I'm on the board. Am I making sense now?"

"But again, of course you can prove—"

"Let me finish, sir, please. You see, Stefan was involved in the grand larceny deal—the theft of diamonds."

"And a murder," Ollie said. "Don't forget that. If he was guilty of the diamond theft, he's tied in with and just as guilty of the murder."

"We can discuss that later. I don't believe the diamonds and the murder are the same case, but that's not the point I wish to make. May I continue?" Without waiting for consent, Chops got up and walked in a small circle, his huge arms behind his back. "Stefan was involved in the theft of the diamonds and was ready to make a full confession."

"And we know the diamonds were never recovered," I said quietly.

"That's because Stefan had them."

"You're positive?" Burton asked.

"Absolutely. He told me. I didn't see them, but I believed him. That is, he told me in such a way that I did not have legal knowledge because—as a good, law-abiding citizen and registered voter in DeKalb County—I would have felt it was my duty to go to the police. But I knew and he knew I understood."

"And the purpose of your last call was what?" Burton asked.

"Stefan was ready to accept any further punishment for the diamonds and to return them. That wasn't even the issue. The issue was the nonprofit organization. He wanted to make sure there was no smear or connection. It's all documented. I mean legally documented to show that it's clean money."

"Okay, yeah, maybe, so tell me about the diamonds," Ollie said.

"I don't know anything except this: He planned to return them."

"Oh, right—of course he did."

"That's what Jason Omore told us," I said, but Ollie acted as if he hadn't heard me.

Ollie started to get up, but Chops still walked around the room in his tight little circles. The detective settled back into his chair. Both of his hands showed slight tremors now. "So Lauber got religion in prison and—"

"Despite your caustic and somewhat negative attitude," Chops said, "such transformations do take place."

I smiled. He was no longer talking like someone

from the inner city. The more Chops talked, the more I liked him; the more he talked, the less I liked Ollie. He talked the way I would have in his place. I not only enjoy being a smart-mouth; I like other smart-mouths.

"Okay, let's move on to the return of the diamonds. How do you know?"

"Simple. I was to be the go-between."

It took a few seconds for Burton, Ollie, and me to react to Chops's statement. "Yes, I was the go-between to return the diamonds. Not to deliver them personally, you understand. I was the go-between to work this out with the police and the insurance company. He had someone else in mind to actually deliver the diamonds."

"And Lauber planned to return the diamonds? Just because he had a change of heart?" The disbelief was in Ollie's voice.

"Yes, because he had a change of heart," Chops said. "Stefan asked me to come here today." He looked at his watch. "Actually, it was to have been at 4:00 today—in less than an hour." He turned his back to us. But I saw the tears spilling out. He pulled out a handkerchief and blew his nose. He walked over to the window as if to stare down at the lake.

"Okay, let's say I believe you—"

Chops turned around. "You believe me, do you? I tell you what I would like you to do, Mr. Viktor. When you go to your home tonight, I want you to get down on your knees, look deeply into your heart, and ponder how little your opinion means to me."

I roared with laugher.

Chops winked at me. "In short, I don't care if you believe me. You didn't believe me when I was innocent of a serious crime; I expect nothing has changed."

"Let's say I believe you," Ollie said. "Where are the diamonds?"

"I have no idea. Stefan didn't tell me. I assumed

they were in his room here at the hotel."

"The room has been searched," I said.

"At least twice and also by the police," Burton said.

"Searched and ransacked," I added.

"Really? What happens now?" Chops asked. "If you don't have the diamonds to return, there's nothing I need to negotiate. Is that correct?"

"Don't leave town—"

"I love it when you say things like that," I said, cutting off Ollie. "It sounds so TVish. Aren't you also supposed to tell him that you expect to be in touch with him?"

"Get out of here," he said to Chops. He turned his back on him and glared at me. "I don't think you like me very much, do you?"

"You're extremely perceptive." I gave him my best smile.

"I'm only trying to do my job," Ollie said. "Give me a break."

Immediately I felt bad for being smart-mouthed. "You're right. I apologize for my rudeness."

"Now what?" Burton asked. "Anyone have any idea what we do now?"

"I think we need to wait," Ollie said. "I expect at least two more visitors before the day is over."

"Who might they be?" I asked.

"Lucas and somebody named Scott Bell-James—"

"Is that the man in 621?" I asked.

Instead of answering me, Ollie said, "I've left messages for both of them."

I didn't want to sit in the room with Ollie and just wait. I decided to take a walk beside the lake. When I announced my intentions, Burton asked if he could accompany me. I readily agreed. Ollie said he had phone calls to make anyway.

Frankly, I also wanted to get away from Ollie for a few minutes. He was quixotic—one minute he acted like a normal person, and then he'd shift and act like a man on drugs who was waiting for the next fix. I didn't think he was an addict, but his habits were peculiar.

The sun was a white ball, and even though it was mid-afternoon and I put on my sunglasses, I still had to squint. Part of the reason was the glare from the lake itself. In the warm afternoon sun, the impatiens were clumps of red, white, pink, and orange. They seemed to peek out from the immense variety of monkey grass and hostas. A small sign boasted of sixty-four varieties of hostas, and I didn't doubt it. I had never seen such a variety in stripes and solids, variegated and in colors ranging from blue-green to chartreuse.

When we reached the SOUTHERN HERB HAVEN (or so the sign declared), I wanted to pause and inhale the fragrances that teased my nose: rosemary, sage, mint, the peppery scent of savory, and the fragrance of sweet marjoram. "Oh, this is wonderful, isn't it?"

"It's nice," Burton said, which made it obvious that flowers and spices weren't high on his list of favorite things.

We moved on down the path and saw a glass-enclosed area of Jerusalem cherry plants. They smell terrible, but they were made untouchable because their bright orange fruit is poison and a part of the foxglove family. I could have stayed all day as we walked among the blue, violet, and white lobelia.

"You didn't come out here just to wander among nature," Burton said. "Something is troubling you. Right?"

"Either you're highly intuitive or you read me well—maybe both."

"Maybe," he said and rewarded me with that gorgeous smile.

"I feel as if there's some kind of conspiracy going on around me."

"Conspiracy?" he asked. "Maybe. The diamonds are worth a lot of—"

"I didn't mean the diamonds."

He stopped and stared at me. "You've lost me."

"You talk to me about God—"

"Yes, but specifically about Jesus Christ the Savior."

"Okay, specifically about Jesus Christ. Then Jason Omore is a Christian, and I learn that Stefan is a believer. Chops Harrison becomes the newest surprise," I said. "Oh yes, and Ollie is one—or at least he's supposed to be one, too."

"You don't think he's genuine?"

"I don't know," I said. "You're the preacher. You ought to know."

Burton laughed. "Long ago I stopped judging people. At best I'm a fruit inspector."

Now it was my turn to look confused.

"Jesus said, 'By their fruits you will know them.' So I test fruit from time to time, but it's still not my job to decide who believes and who doesn't. My role is to encourage and help those who are open. If they are good fruit, I do whatever I can to help them grow."

"I like that," I said. "Great attitude." Immediately I thought of Uncle Rich, who always knew with pinpoint accuracy—or so he implied—precisely which people would enter the portals of heaven and those who rushed toward the pit of utter destruction.

"So about this conspiracy," Burton said. "Want to tell me more?"

"I feel as if I'm getting crowded, that's all."

"Am I pushing too hard?"

"No, of course not." I bent down and pinched the top two leaves off a chocolate mint plant and handed him one. I chewed on my leaf. He watched me and did the same. "But, Burton, it's as if you had programmed each of the others to come in and recite their stories— their experiences of faith—just for me."

Burton stopped walking and grinned at me.

"So now you're going to tell me that it's some kind of divine conspiracy."

"Is it?" he asked.

"Is it?"

"I don't know," he said softly. "I know that I pray for you every day. I want you to experience deep inner peace—the kind of peace I've found."

"You pray for me?"

"Every day."

As I stared into his dark blue eyes, I knew he meant every word. "I don't know, Burton. I think—I think maybe I want to believe all this. Maybe I will."

"Maybe you will," he said, and we continued walking.

We had made a complete circle, which I estimated to be about three-quarters of a mile.

After he said those words, I didn't respond at first. Frankly, I didn't know what I wanted. "Maybe," I finally said.

As soon as Burton and I completed the circle around the small lake, we decided to join Ollie. We had gotten within ten feet of the room when a man came from the direction of the desk. He stopped at the door of the suite the inn had given us and knocked.

Burton stepped up and introduced himself and me. Before he had a chance to tell us who he was, Ollie opened the door. "Come in, come in," he said.

We entered the room, and all three of us turned to the stranger.

"I had a message on my cell that Detective Oliver Viktor wanted to see me. My name is Scott Bell-James."

Although he was probably about five seven, I estimated his weight to be in excess of three hundred pounds. His tan suit pants strained to encompass his enormous thighs. The buttons on his shirt met, but there was no possibility he could button his chocolate brown blazer. He wore a tie of yellow polka dots on a field of rich russet, which clashed with his blazer and emphasized the extraordinary circumference of his neck. His face was extremely round, and his almost-auburn eyes glinted with intelligence. In spite of his great size—or perhaps because of it—he was compulsively neat. His clothes were immaculate. His hands were pink and his nails manicured and neatly trimmed. He looked as if he had just come from the barber, with not a single strand of his graying-brown hair out of place.

He carried a briefcase that he clutched tightly.

Ollie approached him silently and appraised him for several seconds in a way that probably would have intimidated most people. "Yes, Mr. Bell-James. I'm Oliver Viktor." He pointed to a chair and asked the man to sit. "It's really quite a small thing, sir." Ollie sounded as if he were trying to imitate Peter Falk as Columbo.

"Certainly, Mr. Viktor. Just how may I help?"

"You are booked in room 621?"

"That is correct."

"You asked for 623 first?"

"Yes, I did."

"Why did you want 623?"

"Is there a crime against requesting a particular room?"

"Oh no, sir, of course not," Ollie said quietly. He scratched the back of his head. "It is a bit unusual, but not illegal." Ollie's hands were no longer shaking, and he seemed calmer than he had been since we first met.

"But why did you want 623? Why didn't you ask for, say, 519?"

The man stared at Ollie for what seemed like a long time. He blinked a couple of times. "That information is not quite correct. I did not ask for 623."

"Well then, the information I have contradicts that, and this whole thing seems confusing to me," Ollie said.

"No, I might as well tell you. I asked *about* 623—but that was only to verify that Stefan Lauber had that room." He took several deep sighs as if he felt relieved to explain. "If the room had been vacant, then I would have known he wasn't there. I knew he had been there the week before. You see, I, uh, hired a private investigator to locate him for me. Very simple, right?"

"Go on."

"Once the clerk informed me that Mr. Lauber was in room 623—I pointedly asked him, and it cost me a small bribe to get the information—I requested the room next to 623." He held up his hand and said, "I did not explain my reason, and I'm not sure what I would have said if the clerk had asked. He didn't."

"And he gave you room 621."

"That is correct."

"When did you check into room 621?"

"Three days ago."

Ollie sat in silence as if waiting for Scott Bell-James to add more. Outside a mower started up at the end of the building.

"Why did you want room 621?"

"I didn't care if it was 621 or 625. Either one would have been satisfactory." As he spoke, not only was his pronunciation precise, but I detected the slightest British accent.

This time Ollie sighed. "Okay, Mr. Bell-James—"

"Please call me Scott."

"Okay, Scott, why did you want the room next to Stefan Lauber?"

"It is quite simple. In fact, the reason is very, very simple. I came to the Cartledge Inn to kill him."

All of us were so shocked by Scott Bell-James's confession that he came to murder Stefan Lauber that for several seconds we simply stared at him.

Ollie recovered first and said, "You admit you killed Lauber?"

"I did not say that, and I made no such confession." Scott straightened up as if to make his short stature taller. "I came to the Cartledge Inn for the precise purpose of putting an end to his miserable existence. However, I did not commit the deed." He smiled. "I was quite fortunate, because someone took care of that untidy task for me." He walked over to the wingback chair. Without being asked, he sat and carefully pulled the creases on his slacks to avoid wrinkles.

"Okay, I want to be sure this is correct," Ollie said. He pointed to Burton and me, introduced us, and explained who we were. He emphasized that we were not police but we were professionals. He didn't say what kind of professionals, and Bell-James didn't ask. We sat on the couch and turned so that we could face Scott.

Ollie sat on the opposite couch and pulled out the ubiquitous notebook. "If needed, they will act as witnesses to this conversation. Do you have any objections?"

"Of course not. Ask whatever you wish. I have absolutely nothing to hide."

"Okay, let's review this." Ollie went through all the

information Scott had given us and ended with, "You admit you came here to kill him. You were here two nights before the murder, and you claim you did not kill him."

"That is correct. I did not murder Mr. Lauber."

"If you came to kill him," Burton said, "why didn't you do it the first or second night?"

"The first night, Monday, I wasn't ready. Although I am a man of great determination, I am not a person of great courage, you see, and I had to work up the courage—the ability—to commit the deed."

"And the second night?"

"Tuesday night, I was almost ready. I knocked at his door, but he did not answer. I went to the lobby and used a hotel phone to call his room. He did not answer and I left no message."

"Why didn't you call from your room?"

He smiled. "Perhaps I've watched too many episodes of *Law and Order* or reruns of the old *NYPD* series, which was my favorite, but I assumed there was the bare possibility that the Cartledge Inn might maintain a record of calls from room to room. I knew they would not have a record from the lobby."

"Wait a minute," I said. "You've been so open about all this, why were you devious about that?"

"Oh, that is extremely simple," he said. He tugged at his tie to loosen it slightly. "I had not settled on whether to make my crime public. I had planned to shoot him, but I had yet to decide if I wished to go to the police and confess or attempt to hide what I did. That does take considerable thinking, would you not agree?" He stood and took off his blazer. He folded it neatly and carefully laid it on the arm of the chair. "Would you mind if I had a bottle of that water? I am quite parched."

Burton was closest to the cooler, so he grabbed one and handed it to Scott. The man drank greedily. The three of us sat and watched while he finished all eight ounces.

"Would you like another?" I asked.

He shook his head. He laid his briefcase carefully on the floor, walked over to the cooler, picked up a paper napkin, wiped the bottom of the water bottle, and set it on the table. He came back to the chair and sat. For a man of his girth, he moved gracefully. "So what is your next question?" Scott asked.

"Well, perhaps it's too obvious," Ollie said, "but why did you want to kill Lauber?"

"Oh, I apologize, I truly do. You see, I've never been interrogated before. This is quite an adventure. I assumed you knew all of that and that was the reason you had asked me to come in for an interrogation."

"All of that? What do you mean?" Ollie leaned forward as if this were the most fascinating witness he had ever questioned. I wondered what kind of role he now played.

"Permit me first to explain my background," Scott said. "Please indulge me and try to be patient with me. My late wife said that it sometimes takes me a grand loop around Piccadilly Circus before I make my point."

He told us that he was British by birth and an American citizen by choice. He went into lengthy detail to explain why he had a hyphenated surname, and it had something to do with a family named James that was disreputable and it was his father's way to distinguish between them.

I was already bored, but I wanted to watch and see how Ollie handled this. To his credit he said nothing, although he crossed and recrossed his legs three times.

Scott Bell-James told us, eventually, that his wife of twenty-three years had died of cancer a year earlier, and she had been his total life. "Without Edna, I really have little else to live for." He said that during her lingering illness of more than two years, he diverted himself by thinking about the terrible crimes committed by Stefan Lauber and that he ought to be punished "for his dastardly deed."

"But why that crime?" I asked. "It seems, well, so offbeat. I'd think you'd focus on something more— more like rapists or—"

"Again, I need to make myself clear. You see, Edna's brother was Jeremiah Macgregor."

The three of us stared at each other. Ollie raised his hands and shrugged.

"Who?" I asked.

"Jeremiah Macgregor," he said. "May I have another bottle of water?"

We went through the same ritual again, including drying off the bottom of the plastic bottle. After he was seated again, Scott said, "Oh, perhaps you did not know or you did not make the connection. Forgive me. I live with such inner pain and become quite obsessive, and I quite forget that others do not know. You see, Jeremiah Macgregor was my late wife's brother. That may not sound like a strong bond, but I wish to assure you that he was far, far more than my brother-in-law. He was more like my own brother. No, he was more than that. In my entire life, I have never had such a friend, someone who understood me so well, accepted my faults, and truly, truly loved me. I often said he was the brother I never had. For almost twenty years, the four of us spent our holidays—sorry, our vacations—together and were the closest friends."

I was the impatient one this time. I was ready to say, "Stop circling Piccadilly Circus."

He must have read my face. "Please forgive me," he said and nodded my way. "I shall attempt to condense this. Edna and I were never able to have children. Jeremiah and Roberta. . ." He paused and smiled before he added, "Roberta is my younger sister. I have two sisters but no brothers—"

"Yes, we understand," Ollie said.

"Well, this is important, I think. You see, I married Jeremiah's sister, and he married my sister. Is that not rather amazing? Actually, I have two sisters—"

"So you've already told us," Ollie said.

"Oh yes, so I did."

"Just get to the point before I die of old age." Ollie had stopped being Columbo and now segued into a bad-cop routine.

"Yes, yes, of course. But you see, Jeremiah and Roberta have sons—three wonderful boys—and I have had to assume some degree of responsibility—"

Ollie got up, walked over to Scott Bell-James, grabbed his tie, and jerked him forward. "I don't care about Roberta or Jeremiah or their five sons—"

"Three sons."

"Two. Five. So what?"

"Oh yes, but of course that would not matter to you," Scott said. He didn't seem the least bit uncomfortable that Ollie had yanked him forward, although that quick jerk must have hurt his neck.

I got up and walked over. I removed Ollie's hand from the man's tie and straightened it. "Scott, please forgive us for our impatience, but your late wife was correct. You're taking a long time to get to whatever it is you want to tell us. Can you be just a little more direct?"

"Yes, yes, I can do that." He reached for a third bottle of water, and Burton tossed it to him. He drank the contents and thanked us for being so accommodating. As soon as he finished, I took the bottle, and he watched me wipe away all moisture. He rewarded me with a smile.

Ollie was ready to blow up in anger, but I laid a restraining hand on his shoulder. "Why don't you sit back down, Ollie? I'll help Scott tell his story." I got down on my knees next to him.

"Okay, help us with the connection. Who was Jeremiah Macgregor, and what does he have to do with Stefan Lauber?"

"Why, he was the courier. Weren't you aware of that fact?"

"The diamond courier?" Burton asked.

"Yes, of course. That is the reason I have been so— so compulsively antagonized. Edna was his sister, and my truly beloved wife. First I lost Jeremiah, who was my best friend. My best friend in the—"

"Yeah, I know, the best in the world," Ollie said

and let out an extremely loud sigh. "Finally."

I held up my hand to Ollie and said to Scott, "Go on, tell us."

"As my beloved wife declined in health, I realized I would soon be deprived of the two people I loved the most in the world. As her cancer progressed, I became obsessed over Jeremiah's death. Perhaps it was the only thing I could do at that time to cope with her illness. By allowing my mind to focus on repaying Stefan Lauber for his odious crime, I could find a reason to continue to live. Finally, Edna died. I had lost two of the dearest people in my life, my sweet, adorable Edna and my very best friend in—"

"In the world."

Scott stared at Ollie and back at me. "Is he angry about something?"

"He's a policeman and he suffers from acid reflux," I said. "He wants information quickly. Just go on."

"One evening I listened to the local news on the NBC affiliate. I don't like the Fox Channel because—" He stopped and cleared his throat. "That is, I heard that Stefan Lauber had been released from prison. He had served less than two years. Two years for accepting stolen goods—but worse—two years for a crime that included the murder of Jeremiah, my best—"

"Your best friend in the whole world." Ollie rolled his eyes.

"I could think of nothing else—I don't mean that almost literally, you understand, because although most people use that word, they only mean it as a figure of speech that—"

"Yes, it's a figure of speech," Burton said.

"Anyway, I decided I had to have justice. I searched online for a private investigator." He smiled as if pleased with himself. "I remembered how they did such things in the TV shows. I actually interviewed three, but I finally settled on Terrance Waylin. He is local, you see, and his office is located on—"

"Let me see if I can help here," Burton said. "You hired the investigator, and he located Lauber for you. You learned he was staying here at the Cartledge Inn, and you decided to come here, meet up with him, and kill him."

"Exactly. And I must say you are excellent for putting it so concisely. Thank you so much."

I glanced at my watch. Scott Bell-James had been in the room nearly twenty minutes and had given us perhaps three minutes of information. I stayed on my knees and said, "Scott, help us. How did you plan to kill him?"

"Oh, I was going to shoot him. You see, I went to a pawnshop in Avondale Estates. It's at an intersection with a strange name—Sam's Crossing. It intersects with College Street."

"Yes, I know where that is," I lied, but I wanted him to move on.

"You can surely understand that I did not want to go to a regular gun store because—"

"Yes, I understand," I said. "What kind of gun did you buy?"

"The weapon I purchased was manufactured in Switzerland. It is called, I believe, a SIG-Sauer 9mm semiautomatic pistol. It is a compact, short-barreled handgun and holds an unusually large number of rounds in the magazine. Sixteen the man at the pawnshop told me. And unlike most other pistols, it has a double action, which means that it did not need to be cocked to be fired. All I needed to do was pull the trigger. That was why I purchased the SIG-Sauer. Oh, I do not mean because of the bullets, but because I didn't have to do anything but fire."

"Thank you," I said. "Where is the pistol now?"

"Oh, I discarded it. I threw it as far into the lake as I could. I mean the lake here at the Cartledge Inn. I understand that it is more than twenty feet deep, but I assumed there was, is, virtually no likelihood of draining—"

"Okay, enough," Ollie said softly as he paced the room. To his credit, he didn't add anything more.

"Did you ever see Lauber?" Burton asked.

"Certainly. I went to his room Wednesday night—the night he was murdered. I had the gun concealed in my left pocket. I'm left-handed, you see, and I could still knock with my right hand. I thought that was a rather good ruse to—"

"So you knocked!" Ollie said.

"Well, yes, I did. I mean, I tapped on the door, but it wasn't locked. So I pushed it open—"

"And?" I asked.

"Why, he was dead, of course. But you certainly know that, don't you? For a few moments, I was quite upset. Actually, I was disappointed because someone else had brought justice in the world. I didn't know whether to cry or to leap with joy."

"Did you search the room?"

"You must be joking. The room was a complete

mess—all torn up. On TV don't they say the room was tossed? And why would I want to search the room? I went there to kill him, not to steal from him."

"What about the diamonds? Didn't you want them?"

"Diamonds? What are diamonds to me? Diamonds cannot purchase happiness or give peace of mind or provide solace in my grief. No, I wanted only revenge." He stared at me, and his eyes pleaded for me to understand. "Oh yes, and you see, I did resolve the situation. I had decided to go to the police station—I even knew where it was located. Right off I-285 and Memorial Drive. I even made a practice run earlier during the day. I was afraid I'd be so unstrung that—"

"And give yourself up?"

"Not exactly. I planned to write a confession, hand it to the policeman at the desk—I did not go inside, but on TV they always have a desk. Then I planned to stand there and shoot myself in the head. I read that those who shoot themselves in the stomach or the heart do not always succeed, and that would be a great tragedy."

Burton came over and knelt on the other side of Scott. "How do you feel now?"

"Now? I'm grateful I did not have to take his life or my own. But, yes, I would have done it. Yes, I certainly would have. So I believe justice has been served."

"*If* he was involved in the murder of Jeremiah," I said.

Scott stared at me. "Are you trying to say he was not?"

"No, because I don't know," I said, "but I have a

feeling—call it only intuition or a gut feeling—but I don't think he was connected with the murder."

"How can you say that?" Scott asked.

"I was Stefan's therapist."

"And he told you he did not kill—"

"No, we did not go into that, but I don't think he did. He did many wrong things, but I do not believe murder was anything he'd be involved in."

"Yes, but if that—that horrible Willie Petersen did the killing—Lauber would not have literally pulled the trigger, but he would have been guilty."

"I'm stepping out—way out," I said, "but I don't think the murder of the courier and the robbery were the same crime."

"How can you say that?"

"Stefan once said that he had done many wrong things, but he'd never been involved in any form of violence, and he made a point to say that he would never have tolerated it."

"Yeah, right," Ollie said.

I ignored him. "Stefan also said that one time there was a crime of violence in which he was implicated, but he wasn't connected with it."

"And you believed that slime bag?" Ollie said.

"I believed *my client*," I said.

"Oh dear, dear, if he was not in any way involved," Scott Bell-James said, "I might have—I might have committed a crime instead of exacting revenge."

"Yeah, well, I hope that was true—but you have only Lauber's word, for whatever that's worth," Ollie said.

"It's worth a great deal to me," I said. "I believed him."

"How sweet," he said, his voice heavy with sarcasm. "However, as far as I'm concerned, he was a felon. Any man who would be involved in that kind of theft could just as easily be involved in murder. Right now I'm not sure anyone cares whether he was involved. Lauber is dead. The diamonds are still missing—at least we have not found them."

Ollie turned to Bell-James. "Okay, Scott, you may go," he said in a calm voice. "Did you throw away the gun?"

"I said—"

"I know what you said. Did you throw away the gun?"

"No." He looked away. "I was afraid that it might—might implicate me in some way."

"Of course," Ollie said.

Scott picked up his blazer with one hand and his briefcase with the other. He opened the briefcase and held it out with his left hand. "Here it is. You will notice that it has never been fired. That is, I have never fired it, but the previous owner might have. As I explained, I bought it at a pawnshop and—"

"Yeah, whatever," Ollie said and pulled out his handkerchief and took the gun. He laid it on the table.

I smiled as I watched Ollie wrap the gun and lay it aside. It was exactly how they do it on TV. Maybe those shows do have some reality to them. Or maybe Ollie watches them and imitates the detectives.

"Just one more thing," Scott said. "How will I know—about whether Lauber had anything to do with—?"

"It will be on the news," I said. "You said you didn't like to watch the Fox Channel, so you can see it on CBS."

Scott started to give each of us a good-bye, but Ollie stopped him again. "We're glad to have met you and appreciate your forthrightness. If there's anything else, I'll be in touch."

"What about my gun? I certainly don't plan to use it, but I surely would not wish it to fall into the wrong hands. I heard of one case where a policeman took an innocent man's gun and—"

"You'll get it back," Ollie said sharply. "Just leave us alone now." He spoke those last words through clenched teeth.

Scott stared at each of us for a few seconds and hurried from the room.

"Now what?" Burton asked. "So far everything comes up empty."

"Not quite. We still have a few things left to explore," Ollie said.

"Such as?" I asked.

Just then someone knocked at the door.

14

I'd like all of you to meet someone," Ollie said and stood aside while a couple entered the room.

The woman came in first. She was small and thickset, and at first I thought she was elderly. As she stepped into the room, I figured she was probably not more than fifty, but with a face full of premature wrinkles and furrows—a face that had seen a hard life. Her long black hair, streaked with gray, was drawn back into a knot at the nape of her neck. Her lips and cheeks were colorless. A plain, no-nonsense woman, even to her ankle-length black skirt and long-sleeved, high-collared blouse.

The man wore a crumpled white suit. Thick glasses had the effect of magnifying his pale blue eyes into great round hypnotic orbs. He was tall, angular, and hard-faced.

"We are the Boltinghauses, Dennis and Fillis. We were told that we could speak to Mr. Stefan Lauber," the man said. "The clerk at the desk sent us here." He looked around at the two men.

"Oh, this is the man you want," Ollie said. Before Burton could react, Ollie added, "They said they wouldn't talk to anyone else."

"Mr. Lauber? I hate to break in on a meeting, but this gentleman"—he nodded toward Ollie—"said it would be all right."

"What brought you here?" Burton asked.

"Uh, well, we are not used to talking in, uh, well, a crowd—"

"These are my consultants," Burton said smoothly. "I wouldn't discuss any business without them or keep any secrets from them."

"If you're sure." The man looked from Ollie to me and then to Burton.

"Positive."

"Well, sir, this is an unexpected pleasure," the woman said. "We have heard many excellent things about you—"

"Such as?" Burton tried to hide his confused expression, but I knew him well enough that I could see he hadn't fully succeeded.

"Well, sir, you see," the man said and peered through his thick lenses, "the word we have heard is that you have jewelry to sell. Uh, rather expensive, upscale jewelry. That's all I'm prepared to say in the presence of these others."

"We are totally discreet," Ollie said. "You can say we're in this business together."

"Please continue," Burton said.

"It is like this," the woman said. "We hear you have diamonds for sale and you need someone to dispose of them for you."

"Dispose?" Burton asked, and he was now in his role. "And by that you mean—what?"

"You know quite well what we mean," the man said. "We're prepared to, uh, take them off your hands and, uh, sell them—for a price, you understand—and you'll get as good a deal from us as you will anyone else."

"And what price do you have in mind?"

"We're prepared to offer you thirty million dollars."

"Do you have that much? In cash? In what form?"

"Bearer bonds," the man said and smiled.

"Bearer bonds have been illegal in the United States since the early 1980s," Ollie said quickly.

"But not in other parts of the world," the woman said. "And they are like cash."

"I don't know," Burton said, and it was obvious he wasn't sure how to go with this.

"How did you learn about the availability of the diamonds?" I asked. "We haven't sent a message through CNN."

"I prefer not to say," Boltinghaus said.

"I prefer to hear," Burton said.

The couple stared at each other for a minute, and she nodded for him to speak. "Uh, well, you see, there was a certain woman who was supposed to, uh, entice you to sell or give them to her and to meet us by 2:00 today. She did not show up, and, uh, she said she had no other means of disposing of the diamonds—"

"So we decided to see you ourselves," the woman said. "In fact, we can offer you a better price—"

"What is her name?" Burton said. "I've spoken to a number of people."

The couple looked at each other before he said, "We are, uh, prepared to match or better any other offer—"

"Tell me her name," Burton said more firmly.

"Knight. Deedra Knight. She assured us—"

"Deedra Knight is dead," Ollie said.

"A likely story," the woman said. "You only want to hold us up for more money." As she spoke, her words faltered as if she wasn't sure whether to believe Knight was dead.

Ollie held out his badge and identified himself. "What else do you have to tell us?"

"I don't know anything more," the woman said. "That's the truth."

"I can tell you only that Ms. Knight approached us and said there was a profitable deal for us. I have been in the diamond business for more than thirty years, sir, and I assure you that—"

"These are stolen diamonds," Ollie said.

"Oh, well, in that case," the man said, "I'm not interested."

Ollie laughed. "Actually, I know who you are. You own that shabby little jewelry store one block off Main Street in Tucker—"

"Shabby?" the woman said. "I would certainly not call it shabby."

"And you've been implicated in several jewelry-fencing operations," Ollie said. "Go on, get out of here."

They rushed from the room.

As soon as the door slammed behind them, Ollie said, "We've learned one thing from that episode—"

"Yes, the diamonds are still missing," I said.

Ollie smiled—a genuine, honest smile—before he said, "Exactly right. Either the person who killed Deedra has them, or no one has located them."

Maybe he wasn't as much of a jerk as I had thought.

Ollie's cell rang, and he turned his back on us and listened for several minutes. "Hmm. Yes, interesting.

Thank you so much!"

After he hung up, he smiled again. With practice, that smile could be as enchanting as Burton's—well, almost. I might even learn to like the man.

"We may have had a very, very interesting break." Ollie picked up the phone on the table and called the desk. "Craig, would you come down to the room? If you could get someone to cover for you for the next ten minutes, I'd appreciate it very much."

Although I wanted to know what he had learned from the cell call, I knew it would do no good to ask. Ollie liked to be in control—and I understood that. If I asked questions, that would make him enjoy his power role even more. If the circumstances had been reversed, I probably would have acted the same way.

While we waited, I decided to open a bottle of water. I took a few sips I didn't actually want. It was really a nervous gesture to do something while we waited.

A knock was followed immediately by Craig opening the door and coming inside. "Here I am."

"Please come in and sit down," Ollie said. He indicated the wingback chair.

"Did I do something wrong?" Craig asked. He was small and almost elfish. When he sat in the large chair, he seemed even smaller and thinner.

"Did you do something wrong?" Ollie asked.

Craig's gaze went from face to face, and none of us said anything.

"Okay, I took that—that woman's money so she could get into 623. Honest, that's all."

"Really? Is that all?" Ollie asked.

I didn't understand the role he was playing, but he

had shifted into a soft, quiet voice.

"Yeah, sure."

"Your name is Craig Bubeck, age fifty-four. Is that correct?"

"Yes," he said. The wariness in his eyes said he sensed what was coming next.

"And how long have you been employed at the Cartledge Inn, Craig Bubeck?"

"Uh," he said and cleared his throat. "Almost a year."

"And, Mr. Craig Bubeck, what did you do before you were employed by the Cartledge Inn?"

He dropped his head and said nothing.

"Tell us, please," Ollie said. "We're all extremely eager and anxious to know."

"I didn't have anything to do with—with the murders and that stuff." His voice sounded as if it might have come from a child. "Honest."

"Suppose you answer my question," Ollie said, and his voice had become even softer.

He cleared his throat again and picked invisible lint from his uniform blazer. "You know, don't you?" It was a voice about ready to break.

"Yes, Craig Bubeck, I do know. Indeed, I know," Ollie said. He turned from Craig and faced us. "He was in prison for six years."

"Uh, no, only four. The sentence was six, but I was paroled early."

"Oh, forgive me for making such a serious mistake," Ollie said. "I would certainly not want to hold a convicted felon's past before everyone, but suppose you tell my two friends here why you were in prison."

"Armed robbery."

I almost laughed. I couldn't believe that short, thin, frightened little man would have the courage to rob anyone.

"I was only the driver," he said. "I didn't do anything—but, yes, because I was involved, I was equally guilty." He looked up at Ollie and said softly, "I paid for my crime."

"Oh, of course you did, Craig Bubeck, and I won't dispute that," he said. "But tell my nice friends what kind of robbery you and your three misguided friends were involved in."

"Jewelry mostly. It was a jewelry store they held up."

"And there's more, isn't there?"

"I was supposed to—to fence the merchandise." He took a deep breath and said, "Okay, here's the whole story. It started with my brother-in-law. He—he owned a jewelry store near Lenox Mall. He has sometimes done things that—okay, he was a fence. He had connections with an organization in Atlantic City."

"And where is your brother-in-law now, Craig?" Ollie stayed in that sticky-sweet tone.

"Back in the jewelry business. He copped a plea and—"

"Yes, I know that," Ollie said. "When I heard that from my department only minutes ago, can you possibly guess what I thought? Surely you must have known we would learn about your past."

"No, I didn't think you would. I mean, what is there to implicate me? I mean, I only operate the front desk—"

"And have access to the room keys."

"Yes, I do, but I have never, ever used—"

Ollie shrugged indifferently.

"Honest, sir. Never. Not once."

"And there's one more thing, Craig Bubeck. Were you ever away from the desk last night? I mean, even once during your shift?"

"Oh no, I wouldn't—" He stopped. "Okay, I was gone for maybe five minutes." His eyes pleaded with us. "I smoke. It's against the rules. I told the Cartledges that I had quit, but—"

"So you went out for a smoke. Where did you go, Craig Bubeck? To room 623 perhaps?"

"Why would I go there? No, I went out the side door of the inn and got into my car. The windows are tinted, so no one could see—"

"But you had to walk past the elevators to get to the side door. Am I correct?"

"Well, uh, yes, but I didn't—I didn't go to room 623 or to any other room. Honest, I—I—I just went to sneak a smoke. That's all."

"And you want us to believe you, don't you, Craig Bubeck?"

"Yes, of course I do."

Ollie squatted in front of him and said, "I would like to believe you. So here's how I can believe you. You return the diamonds and I'll believe you."

"But I don't have them! I don't know anything about them."

The poor man perspired, and I saw fear in his eyes. I also believed him.

"I'm reasonably sure we can assist you and get you some slack on your new prison sentence because you came voluntarily and gave us information." Ollie stared into the man's brown eyes.

"What are—are you crazy or something? I don't have any diamonds. I don't even know anything about any diamonds. What diamonds are you talking about?"

"You didn't know about the stolen diamonds from room 623?" Ollie asked.

"Diamonds? Is that the reason for the murder?" He shook his head. "I saw on the TV and in the papers about the murder. They said robbery was the motive, but I didn't know it involved jewelry—"

"Not just jewelry," Ollie said softly. "It involved diamonds. Millions of dollars worth of cut diamonds."

"Search me. Search my car." He pulled his keys from his pocket. "Search my apartment. You won't find anything."

Ollie walked around the chair several times and glared at the poor man. Finally, he said, "You know what, Craig Bubeck? I believe you—"

"Thank you—"

"I believe you because I don't think you're smart enough to pull off a job like this. It's too big for a little man like you. You're just too small, too simple, and lack the courage to do anything big."

The words obviously hurt Craig. I saw it in his eyes, and I started to object, but Burton held up his hand to silence me.

This time I ignored Burton. I walked over and touched Craig lightly on the shoulder. "The detective sometimes acts like a bully," I said. "Don't take it personally."

"How do I not take it personally?" he asked. I thought the poor man was going to cry. "He's not a very nice person, is he?"

"I'm sorry you have to go through this," I said.

"Can I go now?" he asked Ollie.

"Do you have anything else to tell us?"

"Nothing. Absolutely nothing," he said.

As I watched his face, I knew he was lying. He held back something. But I understood. If I had been in that chair, I wouldn't even have told the big man my name.

Craig got up and started toward the door. I touched his shoulder. "I am sorry." I lowered my voice and said sotto voce, "We'll talk later. Okay?"

Craig blinked twice.

He smiled.

15

"You acted like a cold, insensitive beast to that man," I said to Ollie. "That poor man."

"I thought it was a pretty good imitation of Rod Steiger in that old flick where he played a Southern sheriff. Did you notice how I continued to use his full name and talked softly and condescendingly and yet with authority?"

"Oh, I noticed," I said. "You were convincing, all right."

"It *was* a little heavy-handed," Burton said.

"Yeah, well, that's how it works sometimes." He nodded slightly and said, "You're right. Sometimes I rush things too much."

I tried to decide if I ought to give him the benefit of a few more words about how much I hated what he did. "You hurt that man. You didn't need to act that way."

"Okay, you're right," Ollie said.

Just then his cell rang, and he opened it and said, "Yes." His hand wasn't shaking, and I realized something rather obvious. When his hands shook the worst, he was harsh and vile tempered. When they weren't shaking, he acted as if he played some kind of role in a film. He was truly a strange man.

After a brief silence, he said, "Send him in. We'd love to talk to him."

Ollie motioned for Burton and me to sit, and he went to the door. As soon as someone knocked, he opened it halfway and kept the other person in the hallway. We could hear only muffled voices. In less than a minute, Ollie returned and a man followed him. He introduced Lucas Lauber, Stefan's older-but-adopted brother.

I was amazed because there was a strong family resemblance. Like Stefan, he was lean and sinewy. Although Stefan's hair was dark, Lucas's hair was a medium brown, neatly trimmed and salt-and-pepper. His features were sharp and economical, as if God hadn't been in the mood to waste anything the day He had edited Lucas's genetic file. He had hazel eyes and a long nose. Although he wore no tie, his expensive dress shirt indicated that he felt more comfortable in that than he did in anything sporty. His suit trousers were charcoal gray with a thin blue pinstripe. My guess is that the suit must have set him back at least a couple of thousand dollars.

"You look a great deal like Stefan," I said.

"Our parents tried fourteen organizations before they picked me. They wanted a skinny kid that would look like his brother. They wanted people to think we were truly birth brothers." He smiled in what came across as deprecating. "I was the right age—six years older—and had the right body style and hair color." He laughed. "But Stefan's hair darkened to deep brunet. Mine stayed a lighter shade of brown."

"Did you like your adopted brother?" Ollie asked.

"Do you mind if I sit down?" Lucas asked and sat without waiting for a reply. "Did I like him? That would depend on which period of time you're asking about."

"Oh, not another long-winded—"

Burton put out his hand. "Mr. Viktor is tired, so

please forgive him." He gave Lucas his heart-melting smile and said, "Tell us about your feelings for the past three or four years and move on to the present." He looked at Ollie. "Okay?"

"Yes, of course," Ollie said. He actually sounded courteous this time.

"It started maybe four and a half years ago, perhaps even five, when I learned that Stefan had cheated me. I'm not positive about the time element, but it was long before the diamond robbery. Months at least. Perhaps a year or even two." He closed his eyes as if he could visualize the past. "I still had my office in what used to be called the Bank of America Tower at Peachtree and North Avenue. Pat Fields hadn't yet become—"

"It doesn't matter," Burton said. "We have an approximate time."

"Your relationship with Stefan. Do you want to tell us about it?" I asked. That's always a good, neutral question for therapists to ask when they can't think of anything else.

"Of course," Lucas said. "The first thing you should know is that Stefan was one of the most insightful, most savvy investors I've ever known. It was as if he could smell good deals." He paused and shook his head. "You've heard of Google, I assume. That was one of the last big-profit deals he ever made. He initially invested a small amount—small for Stefan—of $40,000 and then another $600,000. It made a fortune for us."

"For us?" I asked.

"We were business partners. He was the risk taker, and I was the numbers counter—as Stefan called me. I played safe. I didn't make the huge profits on investments the way my brother did, but I never lost anything either."

"Did Stefan lose a lot of money?" I asked.

"Do you mean on investments or on people?"

"Tell us about his investments in people." Ollie leaned forward. His voice was exactly the right tone to elicit information.

Maybe he's not really so bad, I thought.

Lucas cleared his throat and waved away a bottle of water that Burton held up. "Pam Harty—she was the worst, but there had been a few unwise decisions before. He liked women—perhaps he liked too much variety in women and ran from affair to affair. Several of them cost him a few hundred thousand, but nothing big until she came along. I assume you know about Pam Harty. You do, don't you?"

We shook our heads.

"Really? I assumed you knew everything about her, the affair—sorry, my brother liked to call it the romance—but whatever anyone calls it, the whole thing was an awful situation. So far as I have been able to understand, she was the cause of the problem. He never blamed her; in fact, he refused to say much about her, even though she took him—us—for close to four million dollars."

"And he never blamed her?" I asked. "That seems strange to me."

"No, never. 'It was a weakness in me,' he told me when I confronted him. 'Pam was a thief, but she only exploited that weakness. She didn't cause it.' That's as close to his exact words as I can remember."

"Sounds noble of him," I said.

"That wasn't his reaction when I first learned of the theft. He said that later—much later."

"Tell us a little more, please," Ollie said. "Help us. Explain it to us."

"It starts easy and simple enough. Pam Harty went to work as a personal assistant to Stefan perhaps seven years ago. For the first couple of years, she was the total sponge—the kind of employee everyone wants. She wanted to know everything and was available to take on any job, no matter how trifling. She often said, 'Please teach me, Mr. Lauber.' Stefan loved that, by the way. If anyone wanted to get on his good side, just ask him to teach you. And to his credit, he was an excellent teacher."

"And? But?" Ollie asked softly. "What happened?"

"Pam bewitched him or something. I have no idea how this all came about, but somehow she twisted his thinking. She guided him into making several shrewd deals, very shrewd, I must say that much." He paused and turned to Ollie. "Is that important? If not, I'll go on."

"Oh, please go on," Ollie said. "This is new information."

"We can always come back to any of that if it's important," I said.

"Yes, of course," Lucas said. "I don't know all the details, but Pam totally and absolutely bewitched him."

"In what way?" I asked.

"Without permission—without my express permission—he invested one hundred million dollars in some oil scheme in East Africa. *There is no oil in East Africa.* Because it's part of the rift that begins in the Middle East and continues through the heart of Africa,

some entrepreneurs claimed they had strong indications
of oil. There has never been any oil found there—not
a drop. It was some kind of con game that Pam either
started, played, or cooperated in. She bilked him. That
much is clear. She had an array of falsified documents
and geological surveys. She brought in experts with
thick accents and impressive-looking credentials. They
were all part of the scheme. She bilked him totally.
Then, of course, she disappeared. She left with the
firm's money, which was mine, as well."

"Did you go out of business?" Burton asked.

"For six months I assumed we would, but we did
recover—barely." He shook his head. "I lost almost
everything, but by giving heavily from my own
portfolio, I was able to save the company. Stefan had
taken money that belonged to other investors. And I
mean *taken*. He had forged their names to documents.
I could have made life bad, really bad for him, but I
knew it was the allure of that woman."

"Did you prosecute?"

"No. Stefan did turn over one of his personal
accounts, which helped save the firm from bankruptcy.
Just one, and he could have done more, but that plus the
money I pitched in was enough to keep us solvent."

"You're saying Pam Harty left no trace behind?" I
asked. "You didn't think you could find her or—"

"We did investigate. We hired a firm of discreet
investigators. Apparently she had taken on the identity
of a woman who died in a car accident years ago."

"So you let it drop? You did nothing?" Ollie raised
an eyebrow. "That's a lot of money to lose—"

"I saw no way to recover the money. If word leaked

out that our firm had been taken by such deception, we never would have recovered. In the end I chose to do nothing."

"Okay, so tell us about Stefan," Ollie said.

"Did you ever reconcile?" I asked. "You and Stefan?"

"Well, that's a long, long story."

"I don't mind listening to long stories," I said before Ollie could interrupt.

"Yes, we've already heard a few today," Ollie said. This time he laughed.

"When Stefan was in prison—you know that jailhouse-religion thing? He wrote me a long letter. It was ten handwritten pages, and he asked me to forgive him."

"Did you forgive him?" Ollie asked.

"Absolutely not. I believed he was sorry for the wrong things."

"What do you mean by 'the wrong things'?" I asked.

"I'm sure this sounds strange to you, but he seemed most upset about himself. He had been hoodwinked. He had been taken advantage of by Pam Harty or whoever she was. He had violated the trust placed in him. It was all about him. It was as if nothing else mattered but that he was able to be forgiven so he could clean up his dirty little conscience."

"I suppose that would have been hard to accept," Burton said.

"He had no regard for what he had done to me— the pain he had caused or the months of strain and worry—"

"That was when you received the letter, right?" I asked.

He nodded slowly. On his right hand, he wore a large ring with diamond chips. He twisted the ring several times as he spoke.

"You never reconciled?" Burton asked.

"Later," he said. "Yes, later we did."

"What happened later?" I asked. "Did you forgive him?"

"You mean after he repaid the money he had stolen?"

"He repaid it?" Ollie said. "One hundred million dollars and he repaid it? Hey, come on—"

"No, it's true. That's when I was willing to consider forgiving him."

" 'Consider' means you didn't?" I asked.

He smiled sadly. "He gave me the access code to a numbered bank account in the Cayman Islands. I took out enough to repay everything."

"Those things really exist?" I asked but felt embarrassed. "Sorry, I've read that kind of thing so often in books or seen it in films that I wondered."

"But he paid you back the whole amount?" Ollie questioned. "I find that incredulous."

"Incredulous or not, there was enough in the account."

"Enough? How much was enough?" Ollie asked. "How much was left?"

"I'm not sure that's relevant, but I took out enough to pay me back for all he had, uh, borrowed of mine, after I covered our investors. He had nearly eighteen million dollars left, so he wasn't going to suffer when he got out of prison."

Ollie whistled and repeated the amount.

"He had at least one other account. That was in Zurich. That's all I know, but it would not have been a small amount."

"He must have been a sharp investor," I said. "I mean, really sharp."

"Brilliant. Except, of course, for the incident with Pam."

"Yeah, yeah," Ollie said. "And it's a good thing she didn't get it all."

"He was in love with her," Lucas said. "He was beguiled by her, but he wasn't totally stupid."

"Okay, let's move on," Ollie said, "but I can't believe that crook would have made everything good."

I shook my head at Ollie and turned back to Lucas. "And when did you meet again—in person? I know it was at least once while he was in jail at the state prison in Hall County."

"How did you know we had connected again?"

"Just tell us when." Ollie sounded more like a therapist than a detective. "Please."

Lucas stared at his hands and played with his ring. His head bobbed slightly as if he were arguing with himself. "He wrote maybe three or four times and asked me to come see him, but I refused to meet with him."

"And why was that?" the detective persisted.

"I didn't like my brother. As I've already said, I resented him, and I knew he had never liked me, even from the first days together in our childhood. I was good to him, but I detested the spoiled brat. He got whatever he wanted, and quite often he did so at my expense."

"And as children, what did you get?" Burton asked.

"Leftovers. Always what was left after he got what

he wanted." He looked up briefly and went back into the staring mode before he finally said, "Okay, I really have nothing to hide. I detested him. I didn't shoot him, although at one point I probably would have said that whoever did it might have done me a big favor."

"Because?" I asked.

"Because he got the big inheritance and I received half of what he did. Our parents insisted there was no difference between us, despite his preferential treatment. But when they died—both died in a head-on collision when I was twenty-five—it showed how they truly felt. I was worth half as much to them as he was."

"So shouldn't you blame them and not Stefan?" I asked.

"Blame? I'm long past blame. Try anger. Try—try feeling rejected and unloved and unwanted. That will give you a hint—a bare hint of the pain I felt. Nothing ever hurt me worse than my having to listen to our lawyer read the contents of the will. The amount of money meant nothing, because I was already successful and so was he. By the time he was eighteen, Stefan was already worth three or four million that he had built from a thousand-dollar birthday present from an uncle. So it had nothing to do with the amount. It was the percentage. Dear little brother Stefan never allowed me to forget that he was the favored one."

I felt sorry for Lucas and wanted to say something comforting, but nothing came to me. The expression on Burton's face told me how sad he also felt. Neither of us seemed to know what to say.

"Yeah, right, sad and painful," Ollie said. The words

would have sounded harsh except that his voice remained so quiet, I had to strain to hear him. "So wouldn't that be reason enough for you to kill him?"

"Possibly. I thought of it several times. At one point I seriously considered trying to hire someone to kill him for me. Too impractical. I don't know anyone in the criminal element. But the hatred was that deep."

"So let's fast-forward to the day of Stefan's death," Ollie said. "You saw him that day, didn't you? We know for a fact that you did."

"If you know, why do you ask that question?" It was the most belligerent his voice had sounded. He dropped his head for a moment before he said, "I apologize for that rude remark. Right now I feel as if I'm walking around blindfolded in a maze of emotions." He paused and took several deep breaths. "I have no idea how you found out, but, yes, I did see him."

"Do you want to tell us about it?" Ollie asked.

I smiled. Ollie had learned something about how to proceed.

"I don't *want* to do so, but I will. Stefan called me twice on Monday and again on Tuesday. He begged me to talk with him face-to-face. He *begged*." Lucas actually laughed then. "I never thought he'd ever beg me for anything. It was the first time in our lives together that he had ever done anything except demand."

"So you gave in?"

"Yes, yes, but with great reluctance. We met for lunch at Anthony's on Peachtree. He paid, too." Lucas smiled. "That sounds like a small thing, but it was the one action that convinced me my brother had changed. He had never paid for my lunch—not ever. He used to laugh at me and say the older brother was always supposed to take care of the younger. That had been his joke since I had my allowance as a child."

"What did you talk about?" Ollie stood in front of him and gazed down on the man.

"Oh, mostly about God. That is, he talked about God. Mostly I listened."

"Did you believe him?" Burton asked.

"Hmm, that's an interesting question," Lucas said. "As I sat and listened, I focused my attention on his face. I knew my brother rather well. He had been an excellent manipulator, but as he continued to talk—"

"How did you react?" I asked. "Did you believe he had changed?"

"That's difficult to answer. The best I can say is that I believe *he believed* something powerful had happened to him."

"Was it powerful enough that you believed it was a genuine change?" Burton asked.

For several seconds Lucas stared at Burton as if trying to frame an answer. His emotions betrayed him, and his lower lip trembled. He tried to cover it up with his hand, but that didn't work. He started to cry. "Okay, I did believe him."

"And your feelings toward him?" I asked. "Did they change?"

"Yes. Or maybe—maybe I admitted what I had always felt. This must sound unintelligible, but I truly loved him. I had always loved him. I also hated him— hated him enough to want him dead—back then."

"I think I understand," I said. "I've had clients before with similar feelings."

Lucas made an attempt to smile at me. "I realized why I had refused to see him. I knew—I knew I would forgive him—the way I always did. Stefan had been unethical and—and done criminal things, but—"

"But you loved him, didn't you?" I asked.

Although he made no sound, Lucas cried for another minute or so. He nodded, and when he could trust his voice, he said, "Love isn't logical, is it?"

"Not in the least," Burton said. "Not in the least."

I turned my head, and my gaze met Burton's. I don't think he said those words for my benefit, but in that instant, something strange happened to me—something I wasn't ready to admit. In fact, I wasn't even sure what happened, but I knew one of life's supercharged moments had taken place. I couldn't have explained it if anyone had asked, but I knew it had happened. Later I would understand what *it* was.

"I'm the skeptic here," Ollie said. "Let me see if I understand what you're saying. This younger brother had always been mean and manipulative—"

"That's true."

"And you hated him? At one point you hated him enough to kill him."

"I thought—at the time I thought I did."

"And he buys lunch and you get emotional with all that brotherly love business. I want to believe you," Ollie said, "but—"

"You may believe as you choose. My brother is dead, and I really don't care what you think." A tautness came into his voice, and his body stiffened.

Ollie leaned down in front of Lucas until their noses were perhaps three inches apart. "If you loved your brother, why wouldn't you see him in prison when he begged? I'm just not able to believe you held back because you were afraid that you'd forgive him."

"You don't think he could have such conflicting emotions?" Burton asked.

"Maybe I live too much in a good versus evil world, and that usually means it's white or it's black. I'm open, Lucas, but you have to make it clear."

"I don't think I could make you understand."

"Try me."

"For many years I railed against him and against the way he treated me. He was so—so condescending. In small, understated ways he reminded me that I didn't belong to the family. . .that they had found me in an orphanage and no one else wanted me."

"So you had a motive to get rid of him?" Ollie spoke so quietly it took several seconds for his words to penetrate Lucas's thinking.

"Oh no!" The shock on Lucas's face made me wonder if Ollie was right.

"Sounds like it to me," Ollie said. He stared into Lauber's eyes. "It sounds like the perfect reason to kill him."

"I didn't know how I felt. Intense anger filled my heart. And pain. Rejection, I suppose." He leaned forward, and Ollie pulled back. "Do you have any idea how it feels to love someone who constantly rejects you? To hate someone with deep intensity and yet feel loving and protective at the same time?"

Ollie had the good sense to say nothing. Burton nodded.

"That's the best way I can explain it. You see, I

never knew I loved my brother. Or maybe I didn't want to admit I loved him. I think. . .I think that if I had seen him before—before we met across the table at the restaurant—I would have broken down. I had visited him once in prison, but we had a glass wall between us. I stayed as emotionally cold and removed as I could."

"Okay, maybe I understand," Ollie said. "I'm not sure I do, but please go on."

"I didn't want to love my brother. I wanted to erase any positive feelings toward him. I wanted to hate him."

Ollie straightened up and walked in a small circle around Lucas's chair twice before he said, "So if you loved him so much, why did you shoot him?"

"How dare you?" Lucas said. "I didn't kill Stefan. Whether you choose to believe it or not is of little consequence to me. I know I am innocent." He buried his hands in his face.

I wanted to kick both of Ollie's shins the way I'd kicked bullies when I was a kid in elementary school. That was a mean thing for him to say. I felt confused. Minutes ago he had been calm and perhaps even compassionate. I didn't understand how he could change so abruptly. Was he playing both roles of the good cop/bad cop the way they do on TV?

Ollie pointed to him and said, "But you were registered in the next room—in room 625."

"What does that have to do with it?"

"You registered in room 625 so you could be next door and kill your brother."

"That's insane and irresponsible," he said.

"But we know you used that door to go into his room and back out. Right?"

"Yes, but—"

"What else can we believe except that you went into his room? You shot him and—"

"That's totally untrue," Lucas said. "I'll try this again and hope you can follow me. Or maybe I haven't said it well. After we met for lunch, he talked and—well, I knew he was different. I still held back, but I knew Stefan had changed. I didn't understand what was different, but I knew he wasn't the same. He was warmer. Softer." Perhaps he sensed that Ollie was ready to interrupt him, because he held up his hand and said, "Please. Just listen. Let me try to explain."

"Oh, far be it from me to stop anyone from implicating himself in a crime."

"Stop it!" I yelled at Ollie. "Let him talk."

"I'm a detective," Ollie said. "I'm willing for you to convince me."

"I was—I am registered in room 625. And if you check at the desk, you'll see that the payment for the room is on Stefan's credit card." He smiled at me. "That's what I meant about his change. The old Stefan never ever would have done that. This may sound quite strange, but it was the second thing that convinced me he was not the same Stefan."

"Just because he paid for the room?" Ollie asked.

"Yes, just because of that. You see—"

"Hold it," Ollie said. He picked up the phone in the corner and called the front desk. He asked about the room payment. Then he said, "Thanks, Craig."

"Your brother paid for the room, all right."

I knew Ollie was disappointed to learn that Lucas had told the truth. I wanted to smile and dance around the detective, but I sat motionless.

"Now do you believe me?" Lucas asked.

Ollie did his characteristic shrug again. "I believe *that* part. I'd like to believe it all."

"As I said, my brother wanted me to have that room, and he paid for it. Before that, he begged me to come here to the Cartledge Inn. He wanted me in a connecting room so that we could talk all night if we wanted to and we wouldn't disturb anyone. That's something else. My brother never would have been concerned what anyone else thought. If we made noise, he wouldn't have cared. You see what I mean? Not just his story about his changed life, but he—he had developed a lifestyle that was different from the old Stefan." Lucas stopped, and his eyes pleaded with me to believe him.

I moved over to the edge of the couch, reached over, and touched his hand. "I believe you."

"So do I," Burton said.

"Stefan said he wanted to get everything straightened out. And that he wanted my help."

"And did he straighten things out?" Ollie asked.

"Somewhat. If you check the hotel's records, you'll see that I was in room 625 Tuesday evening, the night before he was killed. We spoke from eight o'clock that night until six in the morning."

"How can you be sure about the time?" Ollie fired back.

"Check room service. We both ate our evening meal in his room. We ordered as soon as I got there. We had breakfast a few minutes before six Wednesday morning. Both of us were too exhausted to talk anymore. Besides, I needed to process what I had heard. So I left him and went into my room."

"Through the connecting door?" I asked.

"Yes, of course," he said in a peevish voice, as if he couldn't understand the reason for the question. "That's why he chose connecting rooms. I shut my door when I slept, because my brother snored."

"And after that?" Ollie asked.

"I slept until maybe 11:00—I'm a bit vague on

the time. I got up, knocked on his door, and peered inside. He was gone. So I shaved, showered, dressed, and drove to the office."

"And you never came back?" Ollie asked.

"No, I did come back," he said to the detective. "And you probably have all this recorded someplace." Lucas explained that he had planned to stay at his office only a couple of hours and have lunch with Stefan, but an emergency came up and he canceled. "The nature of the emergency isn't important to you, but you may call my personal assistant and my associate. Both of them were with me until I left."

"What time did you leave your office?" Ollie asked. I realized he had been writing notes. He held his pen poised as he stood directly in front of Lucas.

"I don't remember exactly, but I think it was about 5:30. I thought I'd get back here in about half an hour, but there was a bad accident at the junction between I-285 and the Stone Mountain Freeway. It tied up traffic and blocked two lanes."

"I can check that, you know," Ollie said.

"I don't care if you do." Lucas got up, walked into the bathroom, pulled a box of tissues out of its container, and closed the door behind him. He must have stayed inside a full five minutes. When he came back, his face was flushed, and it seemed obvious to me that he had been crying. Lucas returned to the chair and dropped the tissue box beside his feet.

"And you arrived here at what time?"

"I think it was about 6:20, maybe 6:25."

"Please be as exact as possible," Ollie said.

"That's as exact as I can remember, but that's not

what you want to know, is it?"

"What do I want to know?" Ollie said.

"I'll tell you. I went into my room. At noon I had sent out an assistant to buy a large box of peppermints— it's something called Nevada Parade. It's made only in Las Vegas, and only a few shops in Atlanta carry it—"

"Forget the candy," Ollie said. "Just tell us."

"But I think the candy shows we had reconciled. It was the first time I had bought it for him since—since he was maybe twelve or thirteen. It was my way of expressing—"

His voice cracked, and I said, "Ollie, leave him alone. I know you're in charge, but just back off, okay?"

"Okay, so tell us at your own pace," Ollie said. He actually smiled at me as if to thank me for the interruption.

"I went into my room, took off my jacket, and with the box of peppermints in my hand, I knocked on his door."

"And? What did Stefan say?" Ollie asked.

He shook his head. "There was no answer. I thought that was odd, because he had called me on his cell earlier and told me that he ordered dinner for 7:00."

"And so what did you do?" Ollie asked.

"I pushed open the door, and then I saw—" He burst into tears, grabbed a tissue, and wiped his eyes. "He was lying there on the floor. Blood all over the place. The room had been torn apart."

"You're sure the room was torn up?"

Lucas waved away Ollie's question and said, "He

clasped something in his hand—a paper. I bent down to pick it up, and then I heard a noise in the corridor. It was the food cart, and it stopped in front of his door. I didn't know what to do. I think I must have dropped the box of peppermints—I really don't know what I did with them—"

"We found them in the room, not far from his body," Ollie said.

"Then you believe me?"

"I believe you dropped the candy on the floor. Go on."

"So I—I reached for the paper in his hands. Purely instinctive, I suppose. I'm not sure why, but I did."

"And what kind of paper was it?"

"Just plain white. When I pulled, it tore. I got most of it—"

"Why didn't you get the rest of it?"

"The waiter. I didn't know if he'd try to come into the room. So I panicked and ran into my room."

"And?"

"I grabbed my jacket, put it on, and hurried out of the inn."

"Did you see anyone? Talk to anyone?"

Lucas shook his head. "No, I don't think so." Then he snapped his fingers. "Oh yes, yes, there was one person. I've forgotten his name, but we had met once while Stefan was in prison. I had gone there to get his signature. We never talked then except in the most formal tones."

"Jason Omore," I said.

"Yes, yes, that's the man."

"What about the paper?" Ollie asked. "That paper

you grabbed from his hand?"

"I stuffed it into my jacket pocket."

"When? When did you do that?" Burton asked.

"I don't know. Maybe in the room." Lucas closed his eyes as if he could relive the scene. "No, perhaps not. I remember. In the hallway—near the reception desk when I met the African. He stared at the paper in my hand, and I was hardly aware that I still held it. That's when I stuffed it inside my jacket pocket."

"May I have the paper?" Ollie asked in a remarkably calm voice.

"I don't have it. I tore it into tiny pieces and threw it out the window of my car as I drove away."

"Why did you do that?" I asked.

"Because I didn't want anyone else to know what— what he had written."

Burton and I exchanged glances.

Both of us knew he had lied. It was the first time I had felt that way.

"Why do you want to lie to us now?" Burton asked. "I believe everything you've said. So does Julie. But you lied just now."

"Why?" I asked.

17

L ucas stared at us as if unsure what he should say.

"Yeah, don't start getting evasive with us now," Ollie said. "You've been very helpful—"

"What would you have done with the paper?" Lucas asked. "I mean, if I had kept it, what could you have done with it?"

"Does it still exist?" I asked.

"Please—indulge me." He looked directly at Ollie. This time I sensed defiance in his hazel eyes as he stared unflinchingly into Ollie's face. "If that sheet of paper still existed and I could find it and show it to you, what would you do with it?"

"How would I know until I'd seen it?"

"Give me the possibilities."

"If it was a confession or something incriminating, it would have to go into evidence."

"But if it was merely something personal? What would you do? I mean, what would you do after you'd read it?"

"I don't know. I suppose I'd give it back."

"One more question." All the time his gaze never left Ollie's face. He peered at the detective as if he were trying to read his thoughts. "If nothing on the page contained anything of importance to you or to my brother's murder, would you return it?"

"Probably," Ollie said.

"That's not good enough."

"If it contains nothing that pertains to your brother's

murder, you can have it," Ollie said. "That's a promise."

"Thank you." Lucas sat quietly as if he were replaying the words inside his head. He got up and walked around the room and stopped at the large window. He seemed to stare at the lake, but his back was to me, so I wasn't sure.

Lucas turned around. "I lied to you. I mean about the sheet of paper. But only about that." He hung his head. "I still have it. I will read it to you, but I won't give it to you. I won't let you touch it."

"Now wait a minute," Ollie said.

"If you want my memory to improve, you'll have to agree."

Ollie looked at Burton and then at me.

Ollie nodded.

"Let's do this." I turned to Lucas. "Bring the paper into the room. You stand right where you are and read it. I'll stand next to you to make sure you're reading exactly what's written on the paper. If it has no direct bearing on your brother's death, you keep the paper. How does that sound?"

He nodded. "You agree, Mr. Viktor?"

"If there's nothing incriminating—"

"I want your word," he said.

"Okay, I agree," Ollie answered.

He looked at us a little longer as if weighing whether he could trust us. He smiled before he pulled out his wallet, took out a single sheet of paper, and unfolded it. The page was raggedly torn off at the bottom, but he had folded it carefully.

"This is, well, almost sacred to me," he said.

Before Lucas began to read, I told the others, "The

words are printed, single spaced, in 10-point serif and continue for five paragraphs. I didn't see a printer in the room, but the place was pretty messed up."

"No printer. No laptop," Ollie said. "I saw a list of contents from the room. My men were very careful not to disturb anything, but they checked every area of the room."

"So he must have done this before 4:30 Wednesday," Burton said. "That's when we knew he was back in the room and called room service."

"Makes good sense." Ollie, notebook and pen in hand, turned to Lucas. "Okay, read it."

"Thank you." Lucas began to read. Stefan apologized to his brother and to the world for his "sinful behavior" (he used those two words) and said he had hurt more people through the years than he could remember. The second and third paragraphs gave a summary of his "born-again experience" and his "entrance into forgiveness and life eternal."

Paragraph four said he was in the process of making restitution for his crimes. He admitted having been involved in stealing the diamonds and that he was going to return them.

The last paragraph read: "A few days after I turned to Jesus Christ, my special friend, Jason Omore, told me to choose a life verse from the Bible, memorize it, and repeat it every day. I have done that."

The tear came just below that, and I saw a partial word: *mans*.

"Now I get it! I get it!" Burton yelled. "Now I understand the 623. The *R-o* and 623 didn't mean room 623."

I stared at him. "What did I miss?"

"He meant *Romans* 6:23. It's a verse in the Bible. In fact, it's such a well-known verse I can quote it for you."

"Then please do it," Ollie said. It was obvious he was disappointed by the contents of the letter. He put down his pad and pen.

"For the wages of sin is death, but the gift of God is eternal life through Jesus Christ our Lord."

"That's it? Just that?" As Ollie said those words, Lucas carefully refolded the page and returned it to his wallet.

"You're saying that's why he was obsessed with 623?" Ollie asked.

"Just because of some obscure statement he read in the Bible?" I said. "I find that difficult to accept. That's not the kind of thing that obsessive-compulsives focus on."

"Who said he was obsessive-compulsive?" Burton said. "It's not obscure, by the way. It's well known, but more than that, Stefan Lauber chose a Bible verse. But not just *any* verse—it was a *life* verse. Life, get it? A verse that he would use and quote often."

"Okay, okay," Ollie said.

I was ready to say, "Whatever," but I decided to keep my mouth shut.

"No, I don't think either of you get this," Burton said. "This is powerful." He looked directly at me and said, "It tells us that Stefan was serious about his conversion. He had truly changed."

Was that a message aimed at me? I wasn't sure, but I wasn't going to ask. Instead, I said, "Do you suppose that's why he was murdered? Not just because he had the diamonds, but because he was going to return them? That way no one would profit from them except the rightful owners."

"That's probably right," Ollie said. "So we have a repentant thief, and that means someone whacked him to get the jewels, right?"

"Do you suppose they got them?" Burton asked.

"Obviously not on the night of the murder," I said. "If they had, why would they have also killed Deedra Knight and—"

"And done more searching after killing Deedra," Ollie said. "That assumes, of course, that it was the same person. The room was worse after her murder."

"And do you think the killer found them?" I asked.

That question hung in the room a few seconds before Ollie said, "Let's assume not. If the murderer found them, we're probably out of luck unless some new evidence turns up."

"But if the gems weren't recovered or haven't been so far," Burton said, "we have two murders and millions of dollars in missing diamonds."

The three of us threw out ideas and theories—a lot of talking aloud that amounted to nothing. I finally turned to Lucas. He still stood by the window with his back to us. He was sobbing softly.

I came behind him and laid my arm on his shoulder. He turned and stared at me. Abruptly he grabbed me and held me tightly. With his head on my shoulder and his chest racked with pain, he cried with great sobs. After a few minutes, he pulled back. "Forgive me. I'm sorry for—"

"Thank you for trusting me enough to use my shoulder," I said.

The gratitude showed in his hazel eyes.

Ollie came toward us, and Burton held up his hand. I couldn't hear what he said to Ollie, but I assumed he told him not to interfere. A few minutes later, Burton brought over the box of tissues and thrust them into Lucas's right hand.

When Lucas finally pulled away, he started to apologize to all of us for being emotional. He tried to wipe the tears off my shoulder. "Don't bother," I said.

He thanked me for not pushing him away. "I loved him. I loved him. No matter how much I tried to hate him, deep inside I loved him." Through tearstained eyes, he said, "When I left his room Tuesday night—Wednesday morning—you know his last words to me? His very last words?"

"We can't know unless you tell us," Ollie said.

I resisted the urge to stuff a gag into Ollie's mouth. "I'd like to know," I said.

"Please tell us," Burton said.

"We had a lot of talk between us, as I've already told you. Most of the time he talked to me about Jesus Christ. I listened, but religion wasn't something our family ever had much interest in. This was all new talk to me."

"And?" Ollie prompted.

"Just as I turned to go to my room, he hugged me. Then he prayed for me. *He prayed for me.* Can you believe that?"

"Yes," Burton said softly. "Yes, I can believe that."

Ollie shrugged.

That seemed just as odd to me as it probably did to Ollie.

"He asked me to make him a promise. The promise was that I would give God a chance in my life. When I hesitated, he added *please*—a word my brother had never used with me before—before our reconciliation."

"So you told us," Ollie said.

"How did you answer him?" Burton asked.

Lucas wiped his eyes, and I thought he was going to cry again, but instead he sniffed back his tears. "I said I would consider it carefully."

"That was all?" Ollie asked. "Did he say anything else?"

"One more thing. He said, 'Lucas, I have been praying for you for several months and for two things. The first is that you would find it in your heart to forgive me. You've done that. The second part of my prayer is that one day we'll be together in heaven.'"

Ollie said nothing, and I couldn't think of anything to say.

Burton impulsively hugged Lucas. "I'd like to continue to pray the second part of that prayer on your brother's behalf—that you'll meet in heaven."

This time Burton got the wet shoulder, and the sobs were even louder than before.

As I watched, something else happened to me. I had felt it earlier, but now it was even stronger.

I was hooked.

I believed, and I had no idea how that had taken place.

Just then Lucas pulled away. Burton turned his head slightly, and our gazes met. It was a strange, perhaps mystical moment.

Burton knew.

He knew I had changed.

18

Lucas asked if he could leave. "I need—I need to be alone," he said.

Ollie nodded and said nothing until after Lucas left.

Burton and I looked at each other. I wanted to say something, but I couldn't put into words what had transpired inside me. So I stared.

He smiled, and that face lit up as it always did.

"Okay, boys and girls, any ideas where we go now?" Ollie asked. He perused his notes, flipping pages.

"Maybe we all need a break," I said. I wanted to talk to Craig, and just as much I wanted to get away from Burton for a few minutes. I wasn't ready to talk to him. What would I say?

"Good idea," Ollie said. "I need to check in with my office and do a couple of things." He glanced at his watch. "I have a minimum of an hour's worth of stuff I have to do, so take your time."

As I turned to leave the room, Burton said, "Mind if I walk with you?" He followed me into the hallway. "Let's talk with Craig."

I didn't trust my voice, so I said nothing. We walked down the corridor, and I couldn't tolerate the silence, but I didn't want to talk about me—about him—about us, so I asked, "You caught that look in Lucas's eyes?"

"I'm not sure what I caught," he said, "but right at the end, just before Ollie let him go, I sensed he either lied or held something back."

I turned and smiled at him. "That's exactly what I meant."

"You know, you're pretty sharp," he said.

"And you know, you're wasted as a minister."

"That's part of what makes a good minister," he said. "We ministers listen and try not to condemn others."

"Sounds like a therapist."

"And we learn to sense when people hold back or when they need to say something."

"Again, like a—"

"And especially, we notice when someone we like needs to talk to us but tries to hide it."

Inadvertently I stopped right then and stared. I still wore those four-inch heels that elevated me above him, so I had to look down at his eyes. "You don't miss a thing, do you?"

He shrugged, and I burst out laughing. It was a perfect imitation of his old college friend.

"Whatever," he said.

"And whenever," I said.

He smiled and arched his right brow. "And that means?"

"It means you're right that I do want to talk to you, but not quite yet. I have a few things to sort out inside my head."

"Maybe talking will help sort them out."

"Maybe," I said. "But not yet."

Burton gave me a quick hug. It wasn't quite the churchy hug, and it wasn't what I'd call a romantic hug. It was what I would call nice.

"I'll take more of them—and longer."

"Whenever," he said and smiled.

~

When we reached the front desk, three people leaned against the counter and five people stood in line behind them. I looked at my watch. It was a few minutes after four. Check-in time.

"We're a little shorthanded today," Craig announced. "My colleague is ill, so I hope you'll be patient."

He said that to the customers, but when I turned to Burton, the uplifted eyebrow confirmed what I thought. The message was for us. I got in line, and Burton stood next to me.

"Excuse me," Craig said a few minutes later and waved at me. "I'm sorry your room won't be ready for another hour, but here's the number." He held up a small yellow Post-it.

I took the Post-it from his hand and read the number. "Thank you," I said. "I'll be back."

As I walked away, I held it up for Burton.

He snapped his fingers. "Of course! I had totally forgotten about them."

Craig had written ROOM 624.

We didn't speak until after we both got out of the elevator. I wondered why we hadn't checked on that room before.

"Why didn't Ollie remember?" Burton said. "It's not like him to miss a detail like that."

"And Craig made it obvious this morning that the rooms on either side were taken and so was the room across the hall. He emphasized that room as much as either of the others. He wanted to tell us something even then."

We reached 624 and Burton knocked. The rooms were fairly well insulated, so we couldn't hear any movement inside—it wasn't that I didn't try. I leaned my ear against the door. I pulled back when I heard the interior lock being turned.

A man gazed back at me. I guessed him to be in his late sixties. His bristly white hair curled thinly across the top of his head and thrust out around his large ears, but his neck was scrawny and wrinkled; his shoulders were slight, and he was about as thin as anyone I'd ever met. He wore a simple sport shirt with vertical lines that made him look even thinner. He might have been five six but no taller.

"I would like to ask you a few questions about room 623," Burton said. "You probably know a man was killed there—"

The man stared at him for a long time, his gaze moving from head to foot. After he scrutinized Burton, he did the same with me.

"Who is it?" called a voice from inside.

"The good cop/bad cop team has arrived," he said.

Before Burton could tell him we weren't the police, I impulsively threw myself into the part. "Look, just move back inside, answer a few questions, and we'll be on our way."

"Do you have some kind of warrant?"

"What TV shows have you been watching?"

The woman, obviously his wife, came behind him.

With nearly white hair, a thin, pretty face, and alert blue eyes, she looked almost as thin as he did and even more wrinkled. She nodded to Burton. "You come inside. We won't talk to the bad cop." She stared defiantly at me. "One is enough, but at least we assume you'll be polite."

"Oh, I'll be very polite," Burton said.

"I'll be at the front desk," I said.

Strange people, I thought as I walked down the hallway. Did I look like someone from the police? Were they just freaked out? It didn't matter anyway. Burton would find out.

I went back to the front desk. Two people were in line. Craig looked up, our gazes met, and he shifted away quickly. I didn't move out of line, and he said nothing. It may have been my imagination, but it seemed that Craig slowed down a little. A man came up behind me to stand in line. I motioned for him to get in front of me. "I'm in line, but I'm waiting for someone, so go ahead."

He smiled and thanked me. I had said the words loudly enough that Craig got the message.

While I waited, one more person came to the line, and I let her in front of me. She wanted only a duplicate key to her room.

I finally leaned against the desk. Before Craig said anything, I blurted, "I don't want you to get into any trouble—please believe me."

"I believe you," he said.

"Tell me what you know. And you were holding back, weren't you?"

"I'd rather see someone get away with a crime than

tell that—that—"

"You don't like Mr. Viktor," I said. "Sometimes he rubs people the wrong way." I focused my attention on Craig and determined not to look away. I wasn't trying to intimidate him, but I wasn't going to let him hold back this time.

"Okay, listen, I get a break in a couple of minutes," he said. "Wait for me in the parking lot." He pointed to the one that he had used for his cigarette break.

"Burton might be coming down before we get back."

"I'll leave a message with my relief," he said and pointed the way.

Just then a man and woman with two children came up to the desk with several suitcases.

I walked outside and waited. I stood among the roses. The day was warm. The late-afternoon light was golden—and utterly mysterious. The sky was partially overcast, so the landscape was dappled with sunshine and shadows. I couldn't focus on the weather. I kept replaying the events of the day inside my head—especially *that* moment. I had to sort that out before I could talk to Burton.

I didn't pace—not in those shoes on that concrete, but I did shift weight back and forth a number of times. Just then I remembered that I had a pair of sandals in the trunk of my car. They didn't match my lime green outfit, but they were soft and easy on my feet. My car, however, was on the other side of the hotel. I didn't want to go over and possibly miss Craig, so I waited.

He breezed though the doorway and said, "Follow me," and walked on. We ambled to the edge of the car park, and he led me to a lovely gazebo. He sat down and pulled out a pack of cigarettes, but he must have read the expression on my face. "Okay," he said and put them away. "I need to quit anyway."

"So please tell me about room 624. Who is that couple? What's the connection?"

"They didn't know Lauber, if that's what you mean," he said. "It wasn't anything like that. I mean, they had no involvement with the theft."

"Okay, so?"

"It's what they saw."

"You mean they witnessed the murder?"

He shook his head. "I doubt that. Look, I'll tell you what I know and then you'll leave me alone and let me puff away on my little cancer stick, okay?"

"So tell me."

"It was about 8:30—just barely dark. The police had stopped harassing everybody. Two policemen were still inside room 623, but that was all." Craig said he had gone out to his car for a smoke. No one was around, so he stood outside the car and puffed. He had barely finished his cigarette when he heard a man and a woman talking. "They walked within five feet of me. I had my back to them, and I don't think they paid any attention to me, but I'm sure they smelled the smoke."

He said they sat inside the gazebo, and he would have had to walk right in their line of vision to get back to the inn. "If the Cartledges learned I still smoked, they'd fire me," he said, "and I want to keep this job. It's the first real job I've had since—you know—since—"

"Yes," I said simply.

According to Craig, the conversation between the couple went like this:

"But what do we do? Just—just keep our mouths closed?" the woman asked. "I'm frightened."

"What else can we do? You know from those television shows what happens when witnesses speak up."

"But those are made-up stories," she said.

"Made up, all right, but they're made up from real events," the husband insisted. "Haven't we heard enough times that the story is based on real events?"

"So if we say nothing, then what?" the woman asked. "Does he get away with it? I mean, if he truly did it?"

"Aw, c'mon, they always leave clues and make mistakes. Haven't we seen that a thousand times, as well?"

"So you mean we say nothing."

"Yes, that's exactly what I mean."

"Maybe that's the best," she said.

"Look, I'm scared, too. How was I to know that just because we stepped out of the room when we did—"

"I suppose," she said. "And if we speak up, who knows how long they'll make us stay in Georgia. I want to get home—"

"He said to stay two more days as we had planned and then we could go and we would be safe."

"Yes, yes," she said. "But if police officers come to our door—"

"Then we'll deal with it," he said.

"That's all I heard," Craig said. "They got up and started

to walk away from the gazebo. They were probably going to go inside through the other entrance to the grounds over by the lake. It's well lighted at night."

"So you went back to your desk?" I asked. "And you never said anything to anyone?"

"Are you crazy? Why would I do that?" Craig said. "If that Mr. Viktor had been a little nicer to me, maybe I would have told him, but he's like some of those tough criminals I met in prison. It's safer and better to stay away from them."

I didn't say anything. His fear seemed a bit irrational to me. But if I were a skinny little guy like him and had been in prison among brutish, tough men, I might have been a little more fearful, as well.

He got up from the gazebo. "That's all I know—honest, it is. Please—"

"Please what?"

"Can you tell that detective the truth without implicating me? Maybe—maybe you could mention asking the people in 624 if they heard or saw anything."

"Burton is with them now." I didn't want to go through what had happened, so I said, "Whatever he finds out, we can tell Oliver Viktor."

"Okay, that's all right, I guess," he said. "I just want this to end."

"Me, too," I said.

19

We got back to the desk, and Burton still hadn't come down. I told Craig I would walk along by the lake and he was to tell Burton he should join me. I went immediately to my car and exchanged my heels for the sandals. The relief was immediate. Okay, so they didn't match my outfit, but I didn't care. The comfort was worth it.

Besides, after that hug, I didn't think he'd focus his attention on my feet.

Now I was ready to walk. I don't know how long I walked or how far. The day had cooled off, and the sun's rays hid behind the clouds. Other than that, I paid no attention to anything around me, because I became absorbed in my own private world. I should have focused on the crime and trying to figure out who murdered those two people, but something else troubled me.

"I've become one of them," I said to myself. "How could such a thing happen?"

I had become a believer. Just like that. That experience didn't make sense to me. How could it just happen without warning or a conscious decision? No one had used any arguments or tried to prove anything to me. I just believed. It felt strange to think that way.

"There really is a God—a God in whom I believe." Immediately I thought of Uncle Rich. I figured my experience would upset him, because I believed without going down to the front of the church and confessing my sins to everyone.

The closest parallel that made sense to me was my learning Spanish. In college I had signed up for Spanish as my required language course. I didn't get the language. I did the exercises faithfully and memorized the words. I learned to parrot everything the instructor and anyone else in the class said. About two weeks before the end of the first year, I groaned and knew I could never pass the final exam. It was like memorizing math formulas.

About a week before finals, I sat in the classroom, groaning miserably while the teacher read us a short story completely in Spanish. As I listened, I understood—just like that. It was as if the language suddenly made sense. I no longer had to translate word by word.

"Is that the way Christianity works, too?" I asked myself. "At least for me, is that it?"

Just as I decided that it was, another thought hit me: Did I truly believe, or did I think I believed so that I could be more attractive to James Burton? "Am I that self-deceived?" I whispered.

"I don't know," I answered myself, but I did know. I liked Burton—a lot—maybe even more than a lot. Yes, I did love him, but my sudden faith in Christianity was quite apart from that.

"It is, isn't it?" I asked.

I felt as if I had awakened from a daze. Peace filled my soul, and I don't recall ever having felt such tranquility at any time in my life. "This is real," I whispered to myself. "This is real."

———

Burton hadn't sought me out on the walk, and I finally

went back to the front desk. Craig was busy with a check-in, but he shook his head. "Haven't seen him."

That meant he was still with the couple in room 624. I thanked Craig and decided to go back to the room the hotel had given Ollie to use. When I opened the door, I could see Ollie Viktor standing in the bathroom. He had injected a needle into his arm.

I must have cried out, although I wasn't aware of anything except a feeling of immense shock.

Ollie turned. He looked up and stared into the mirror. He saw my image and finished injecting himself. He cleansed his arm, rolled down his sleeve, put the medication in a small case, and walked into the room where I stood.

"Shocked?" he asked. "Don't be. It's not an illegal drug, and I'm not an addict. It's called medication."

I didn't know if I believed him, so I said nothing.

"Perhaps you noticed the tremors in my hands. They come and go. They're usually the best sign to tell me when I need a shot. Usually one in the morning and one at night are enough for the day."

"Usually?" I asked.

"Most days."

"I assume you've injected yourself several times today—"

"This is my fourth," he said matter-of-factly. "When I'm under intense pressure, the med seems to wear off quicker."

"Want to tell me the problem?"

"I wish I knew. So do my doctors. The problem is that no one knows for certain. I've been tested for Parkinson's disease, or as we call it, PD, and that seems to be the best explanation so far. In two weeks I'll have a brain scan, and that should help." He explained that PD is a motor-system disorder and is difficult to diagnose. He had only one of several telltale signs: trembling hands. He said that sleep problems were common and he had begun to experience some of them.

"So what were you taking?"

"Artificial dopamine," he said. "It's an experimental drug. So far it hasn't produced any positive results."

I nodded, not quite convinced, but open to believe him.

"Another thing is that you may have noticed my mood changes. That's not a common symptom. I get irritated easily or depressed. I can't help it. I know I've made you angry—"

"Yes, yes, you have."

"Please believe me that I can't help it. It—it just happens." Those green eyes stared at me with such intensity I no longer doubted his word. He explained that the symptoms had actually gotten slightly better during the past two weeks. "Until today. I think the tension—you know—made me need extra meds."

"Okay, then what can I do to help? You haven't been particularly nice to some of—"

"I've been a jerk. Don't you think I know that?" Before I could respond, he took my hands in his. "Please try to understand. Right now I feel fine. Why shouldn't I? As you observed, I just injected myself. I have no idea when it will wear off. When I feel the symptoms start to return, I tell myself I won't get angry or yell or—"

"I'm sorry. Honest."

"Help me, Julie; help me. When you see me act weird, just tell me to shut up. I'm not sure it will work, but when Burton did that, somehow I was able to calm down."

"You can count on me to tell you to shut up," I said. In spite of myself, I began to laugh.

Ollie laughed, too, and released my hands. "Hey, I don't know if I like giving you blanket permission—"

"Oh, I'll use it wisely," I said and laughed again. "Or at least I'll use it whenever I don't like what you say."

"Thanks," he said.

His voice was soft—in fact, so soft I don't think I'd ever heard him speak quite like that. He melted me, but then, I'm a sucker for a soft voice. His eyes moistened, and that slapped me down even further.

We looked at each other in silence before I asked, "Does Burton know?"

He shook his head. "Outside of my doctor, you're the only one. Please don't tell—"

"I'm a professional, remember? You don't have to ask me not to tell Burton or anyone."

Almost as if we had planned it that way, a soft tap came at the door. I turned toward it and it opened. Burton walked inside.

"Hey, there's our man," Ollie said. "Now we can get some things done with you back on the job!"

"Yeah, I think you're right." Burton laughed—maybe it was slightly forced, but it was a laugh.

I stared at Burton and tried to read his face. Sometimes it's easy to do that, but he can also be inscrutable when he wants. This was one of those times.

"What do you think we ought to do now?" Burton asked.

The question hung in the air.

Just then I looked up and saw Jason Omore stroll past our room. He didn't know we were in that room, and he didn't look our way.

"I'd like to talk to Jason again," I said.

"You think he knows something he hasn't told us?" Ollie asked.

"I think—I think we didn't ask the right questions." There it was again—one of those far-out statements and I had no idea how I knew it. I suppose that's part of why my colleagues say I'm a good therapist. I listen to that inner prompting, to my gut. As a therapist, I don't get it often, but I listen. In fact, this had happened to me more since coming to Cartledge Inn than it had in the past six months.

I hurried out of the room, and both men followed me. As I exited the building, I saw that Jason had gone about a hundred yards ahead of us. Wearing my sandals made it much easier to walk. If there hadn't been two attractive men behind me, I probably would have run.

"Jason!" Burton called.

He must not have heard his name the first time, but I walked even faster. About thirty feet from the African, I called his name.

Jason turned, saw me, and stopped. Even from that distance, his smile was as big and as genuine as ever. He walked toward me and greeted me with his arms raised shoulder high, as if he intended to welcome me with a hug. "Good doctor, it is my distinct pleasure to see you again." He waved to Burton and Ollie, who were both less than ten yards behind.

"How are you?" I asked.

"That is not a good question," he said. "In our country we would not say that so quickly."

"How would you say it?"

By then the two men had caught up with me and heard our conversation.

Instead of answering, Jason turned and looked heavenward. Pale clouds had drifted across the sky, and the first hint of sunset had appeared. A mild breeze brought along the fragrance of magnolia blossoms from a nearby tree. I inhaled deeply.

"In our country—in the region we call South Nyanza where I grew up—the people are still what you could call primitive. When someone dies that we love, we mourn, but we do it differently." He told us that every evening at dark, the family and friends gathered. They wept and cried all night long. So many people would be present, someone would always be crying aloud. "We do that for thirty nights."

"And after that?"

"After that we return to our lives again. We have mourned, and we have emptied ourselves of our pain. I wish to do this for my friend, but I can only carry this heaviness in my heart for now." He stared at me and said softly, "You Americans seem to think it is a serious weakness to mourn for an extended period."

Before Ollie could interrupt, Jason said that he had been in his room. "But, alas, my heavy heart is such that I have not studied. I can think only of my friend. I have already mingled many tears over his Bible."

"*His* Bible?" I asked.

"Yes, the Bible that belonged to Stefan."

"What are you doing with it?" Ollie asked. "If it's his, did you steal it from his room?"

"And why would I do that? Did he not give it to me?"

I wondered if this was the time to tell Ollie to shut up. I glanced at his hands and saw no tremor.

Burton all but pushed Ollie aside. "Tell us about the Bible, Jason. Why did he give it to you?"

"*Akiya—*" He stopped. "Sorry, that is my own language, which means, I do not know. Truly, I do not."

"What did he say when he gave you the Bible?"

"Ah, that. Yes, that was a bit strange, was it not?"

"In what way was it strange?" Ollie asked.

"He was afraid, I think. Yes, he was very much afraid."

"Of what?" Ollie yelled. "Afraid of what?"

"Of that, I do not know."

"Don't give me that kind of—"

"Ollie, Ollie, take it easy," Burton said. "Let's find a place to sit down and let Jason take whatever time he needs to explain this to us." Ollie started to protest, but Burton added, "We have four African families in our congregation. I've learned that they operate out of a different time zone. If we're patient and listen, we'll learn."

"And what's ten minutes more or less?" I asked. I looked at Ollie and hoped my eyes gave him a warning.

Ollie raised his hands in surrender. "Okay."

Jason led us away from all the buildings until we came to a small promenade that overlooked the lake. It was the highest point of the grounds, and the lake was perhaps thirty feet below. Five leather-cushioned folding chairs were grouped in a semicircle. We sat on the padded seats, which were amazingly comfortable.

"I want your help," Ollie said to Jason. "Please tell me whatever you know. I get a little impatient at times—"

"Yes, that you do," Jason said without obvious rancor, more as if he stated a fact. "Is this not a beautiful site? Is not God's creation special for us? Is it not one of your sayings that we should pause to smell the flowers?"

"Stop to smell the roses," I said.

"Ah, yes, so it is." He had been looking around at the lake, and I thought how naturally he blended in with the quiet setting. He turned his chair so that he could see all our faces. "Now my soul is calm once again. I am ready to speak."

We waited several seconds. From behind me two birds called and sang to each other.

"My friend Stefan knew someone wanted to kill him," Jason said simply.

"How did he know that?" I asked. "Was he threatened?"

"To that question, I do not have an answer. He said to me, 'Someone will make an attempt on my life.' When I asked him for more explanation, he said, 'Do not be upset. I am not afraid of death.' "

"He really said that?" Ollie asked.

"Oh yes, but of course. Even if he had not said

such words, of this I am sure that he was at peace. He had only one major concern. It was the one thing he felt he must do even if his life was in danger."

"And that was?" I heard a slight irritation in Ollie's voice, but I let it go.

"It was. . ." He paused and thought. "It was, as you would say, he was obsessed with his mission. He was learning our language, and he did not know many words, mostly nouns, but his favorite was *almasi*."

"Which means?" Ollie jumped ahead and asked before Jason had a chance to explain.

"Oh, it is the word for 'diamond.' You see, he sometimes spoke to me in public. He wanted no one else to understand, so he used *almasi*."

"So he was sure someone would try to stop him from returning the diamonds," I said. "Why else would he do that?"

"That is true," Jason said. "He feared that someone would kill him before he could return the diamonds to the proper owners." He dropped his head and said softly, "And he was correct, and I did nothing to help. I could have stayed in his room perhaps."

"He told you that?" Ollie asked, interrupting the African's reflective mood. "I mean, about returning the diamonds? That it was the important thing he had to do? Are you sure he didn't plan to sell them?"

"Sell them? Why would my friend choose to do such a thing?"

"For money—a lot of money," Ollie persisted.

"No, that is not true. Not ever would he do such a thing."

"Are you sure?"

"But of course. Would I lie to you? Sir, am I not a Christian?"

"Okay, okay, I got it," Ollie said without conviction. "You say you're telling us the truth, so tell us more."

"There is but one thing I must tell you, and I do not know this is so, but it is what I have come to understand." He paused and wiped his eyes with his hand. "I loved him very much. It's most difficult to speak of him. Never have I had a friend whom I have loved so much." He pulled a handkerchief from his pocket, and we waited until he was ready to speak.

The sun had begun to slip behind Stone Mountain, which was to the west. As I watched, it looked as if the sun had begun to melt into the mountain itself and cast rays of pale orange and purple across the skyline. Below us I heard the first cicadas tune up their nighttime instruments.

"What I do not know is the name of the person my friend feared. Perhaps there were many or only one; I cannot say. I do know that Stefan felt there was one special person—one man who wanted the diamonds. It was a man. Of that I am sure. He was involved in some way with the taking of the *almasi*—the diamonds. The man who carried the jewels was supposed to have given them to one man—Peters or some such name—"

"Petersen," Ollie said.

"As you say. That was a man who would be suspected because he had robbed before, you see. That act was planned carefully, and this I know from my friend. That man, the one called Petersen, gave the bag of jewels to the woman, and she was to take them to my friend. He would dispose of them. Does that not sound simple?"

"Very. So what's the problem?" Ollie asked.

"I can't think of the English, but something happened. It is like putting two crosses together."

"Double cross?" I asked.

Jason rewarded me with a huge smile. "That is the expression, yes. The double cross."

Slowly Jason told the story. He didn't know the name, but a man had instigated everything. He was someone who had influence and knew many people, but also, in Jason's words, "a man of bad character." This man set up the entire operation and used the woman named Pam Harty to work on Stefan. "You see, to have the diamonds was not enough. It had to be someone who was wealthy and influential enough to sell the stones and not to arouse suspicions."

"And that's where Pam Harty came into this, right?"

"Oh yes, she was an evil woman—I met her but once, you understand, but those are the words of Stefan. The one who planned all this—and the man's name I never heard, and I do not think Stefan knew—hired the Harty woman. She spent many weeks, perhaps months, deceiving my friend. He talked many times about being a fool for letting that woman lead him into such a wicked venture."

Now it made sense to me. I had liked Stefan, and he seemed like a man of great common sense. That's not something changed by a religious experience. But if the woman stayed after him and used her charms constantly, okay, now I could understand. His brother had mentioned that Pam Harty had influenced him, but that hadn't really sunk in until now.

"So here is the way it was to work. I mean the way

the double crossing was supposed to work. The courier was to have two containers—pouches or something—and they were to be identical. One of them contained the real diamonds and the other the imitation. In the airport parking lot, he was supposed to be robbed at gunpoint and surrender to Petersen the imitation. He would later hand the real ones over to the one who planned everything."

"How was the transaction to be made? With that man?" I asked.

"Hmm, on that I shall have to think. Did he not tell me while he was still in prison? It was long ago." He turned his face upward and stared at the sky for a few seconds and then closed his eyes.

Ollie sat motionless, but his attention was fully on Jason.

"Yes, I do now remember. It was an *askari*—a policeman. Yes, that is how it was to work."

Instinctively my gaze shot to Ollie.

"Hey, we have hundreds of police in the area. I'm only one, so don't convict me because I'm of the same occupation."

I nodded. Of course he was right.

Petersen, Jason told us, used a gun to hold up the courier—Jeremiah Macgregor. A briefcase was strapped or chained to Macgregor's arm, and Petersen forced him to take out the pouch of diamonds; then he ran with it. As it turned out, Macgregor became so frightened by the robbery that he panicked and inadvertently handed

Petersen the real diamonds.

As he had been instructed, the courier called the police about the holdup. The policeman who planned the event was on the scene or nearby. That wasn't clear except that he would be the first official on the scene. Jason said he thought the policeman would say that he was off duty and had been visiting friends near the airport. The robbery took place in the long-term parking lot of the airport in Atlanta. He arrived before anyone else and grabbed the second pouch. He must have looked at the contents, or maybe Macgregor blurted out what had happened. Regardless, the policeman shot the courier, jumped into his own car, and drove away. Jason could not verify that part except to say that he knew there was a woman with the policeman.

"How do you know that?" Ollie asked. "Lauber wasn't on the scene, and you surely weren't there."

"The woman came to see Stefan. Perhaps two, maybe three days before the murder. She asked for a—a cutting—a portion—"

"A cut?" Burton asked.

"Ah, yes, again. At times my English fails, does it not?"

"And?" Ollie asked.

"Oh, he refused. I was there."

"You were there?" I asked.

"Yes, she visited his room and I was present. We had begun to read the Bible together and pray. Her knock at the door interrupted us."

"Please tell us everything," Burton said. "Don't leave out anything."

20

This is the story Jason Omore told us:

Each morning, did I not go into my friend's room? And to some it sounded perhaps strange, but I conducted Bible study. I did not know everything about the Bible, but I taught him what I knew. Some days we read short portions from other books, but we always read at least one chapter of the Bible together. Sometimes I would teach him the African words if he wanted to know.

I also taught him to sing some of our songs. His favorite was called "Maler, maler ni jogo," which in English means "Holy, holy are the people," and it refers to those people who follow God.

One morning—it was last week, but I do not remember the exact day—we were ready to pray together when a knock came at the door. Stefan and I had been on our knees beside his bed, so we both got up, and he walked to the door and opened it.

"Well, this is quite a surprise," Stefan said. "You're probably the last woman on earth I expected to see at my door."

"May I come in?"

Before he could say anything, she pushed the door open wide and entered into the room. Truly, she was one of the most beautiful women I had ever seen in my life. Her skin was what I would call flawless—not a blemish anywhere, and she wore little makeup. She was so beautiful that makeup she did not need. She had light-colored hair—blond—and she wore it long so that it broke over her shoulders. I know nothing of expensive clothes, but Stefan did and he stared at her.

"You must observe what my money has done for this woman," he said to me. "She has invested it well because she has invested it in herself. She was bewitching before, but she is even more so now."

He pointed to her pale blue suit. "This is by Chanel, and the handbag is Hermes, or is it Prada?" He nodded to the woman.

"Hermes," she said and smiled. "Oh, Stefan, you are magnificent and knowledgeable and so—so gracious."

"Look at the shoes, Jason," he said and pointed. "Those pumps look quite ordinary to you, but I assure you they are not. Charles Jourdan, obviously, at a cost of at least five hundred dollars. She would never use an imitation." He stared at her hand. "Chapard? Is that truly a Chapard watch?"

"But, my dear, you taught me to value the valuable," she said and smiled. Her smile made her face even more radiant. I think that is the word. But the eyes were sad. They were light blue, almost the color of her suit. If the eyes are the way to enter into the soul, she was sad and a truly poor person on the inside.

She walked around Stefan's room, picked up the Bible from the bed. "I heard you had begun to read such literature," she said and tossed it—how do you say—carelessly?

She stopped and stared at me as if she had not seen me before, but I knew she had taken in my image when she entered the room. She stood before me and observed me carefully. She stared at my shaved head and slowly traveled down to my sandaled feet. "Is this a waiter? He isn't properly dressed for the job."

"He is my friend. He is Jason Omore."

"How nice," she said and smiled at me. "Now you may leave."

I said nothing and began to walk toward the door.

"He stays." Stefan put his arm around my shoulder. Stefan was a tall man, perhaps as tall as Mr. Viktor. I started to pull away, but his hand held me.

"I want to talk to you," she said softly and went to sit down. She did not stop the smiling all the while.

"So talk."

"I have personal things to discuss with you, Stefan. Very, very personal things."

"This man is my brother, my soul brother. I have known him for many months, and I trust him as I have never trusted another person in the world. I have no secrets from him." Stefan released me, walked over, and sat on the edge of the bed. He indicated he wanted me to sit in a chair.

As he said those words, I felt my face grow hot. I had not known he felt about me in such a good way.

"Get rid of him anyway."

"I think not." He walked over to her. "You see, he has gained my friendship. My trust. He is one person who will never betray me or deceive me. I have trusted him with my life, and he has proven faithful."

"And I haven't?" she said. "You're right. I was weak, Stefan. Weak and afraid, so I ran out on you."

"No, you ran because you thought I had the paste diamonds."

"That, too, I suppose," she said, "but I was confused and. . ."

She stood up and hugged him. Even in her stiletto-thin heels, she was perhaps four inches shorter.

Stefan was tall, lean, with very dark brown hair and hazel eyes. Momentarily he embraced her. "Hmm, you no longer use Jean Patou fragrance."

"This is a designer perfume. Supposedly designed just for me, and no other woman in the world has a fragrance quite like it."

Stefan slowly pushed her away. "As it should be. No other woman in the world. Yes, I think that's a good description."

She reached for him again. "I've missed you, Stefan. Truly I have missed you."

"How nice," he said. He turned to me. "You have never met Pam Harty, but she was my one true love, the woman who loved me just for myself and promised to stand by me no matter what." He smiled slowly and said, "After she put her hands around millions of my dollars, she moved on. And now she's back."

"You make me sound so—so awful," she said. "And I admit I have been terrible, but I want to change that. I'm different. Truly I'm—"

"Enough." The tone wasn't angry, but it was firm.

She stared at him as if not sure what to say next.

"So why did you come back?" he said. "You walked away with a fortune in cash—a very, very large fortune."

"And I was quite unwise in the men with whom I associated. Two of them in particular were thieves. Can you believe it? They conned me out of my money."

Stefan laughed. I wasn't sure why it was so humorous, but in our culture, we do not believe it is polite for one person to laugh alone, so I joined him in laughing.

"I despise you," she said to him. She no longer seemed aware that I was in the room. Or perhaps she did not care. "You are a thoroughly despicable man." Her words were harsh, but her voice remained soft—the way a woman speaks to a man whom she loves or wants him to think so.

"That, my former truelove, is honest," Stefan said. "Your tricks won't work again, so don't waste the energy. Tell me why you came to see me."

"Isn't it obvious? I came about the diamonds." She seemed suddenly aware again of my presence. She cocked her head toward me. "Please, tell him to go."

"If one of you must leave, it is not my friend, Jason."

"I came to talk to you about the diamonds—the ones you still have."

"Sit down if you like," Stefan said, "but my friend stays."

"I will leave," I said. I did not feel comfortable with such conversation.

"No, stay, please."

"Your choice," the woman said. "Okay, I know you have the diamonds. The word has circulated that you are ready to dispose of them. I want a cut. It's that simple."

"And if I refuse?" Stefan said.

"I hope you won't be that foolish. You know what happened to Petersen and to Macgregor. Such sad things happened to other people, as well."

With lightning-like speed, Stefan grabbed her arm with one hand, her bag with the other, and rushed her to the door. "Don't ever come back. You will never get another cent from me."

She tried to say something, but Stefan slammed the door in her face.

After she left, Stefan said he wanted to pray alone—and I left him. That is all I know about her.

Jason had told us about his meeting with Pam Harty. Although it had been interesting and I had a clearer picture of the woman, he had said nothing particularly enlightening. I wondered if I had wasted my time in wanting to talk to him. I had been so sure he had something of value to tell us, but perhaps I had been wrong. I started to get up and walk away.

"Why is your face like that of the donkey?" Jason asked. "You are much sad. Did my information displease you?"

"Oh, not at all—"

"She means she expected more," Burton said. "She felt we hadn't asked you the correct questions and you had things to tell us—information that might help to solve the murder of Stefan."

"But I did not tell you everything," Jason said softly. "Is there not more for me to tell?"

21

Ollie had listened but said nothing. I glanced at his hands, but they were inside his pockets, although he moved his legs in a slight kicking motion. I wasn't sure, but I suspected the tremors had begun again.

"Please, Jason, will you tell us?" I asked. "I'm not even sure what questions to ask, but I feel you know things that we need to hear. Please."

"Yes, I can do that," he said. "Yesterday Stefan and I were again together in his room. We had spent more than our usual hour in reading and studying Romans—chapter 12. He was puzzled by one statement that said to consider others better than yourselves."

"Is this important?" Ollie asked. He pulled his hand out of his pocket. The tremors had returned.

I put my index finger to my lips. "Be patient, Ollie."

Ollie got up and paced the area. I didn't know if that helped or not, but as long as he was quiet, it would be all right.

Jason told us that a woman came to the door. At first I thought he meant the same woman as before, but then he explained that the two women looked nothing alike.

What he remembered most vividly was that she held a gun in her right hand, and it was pointed at Stefan.

"The woman looked at me then," Jason said.

"Get him out of here!" she shouted.

"I went through this once before," Stefan told her.

"I wonder if women coming to my room will be a usual affair."

"Get rid of him."

"No. He stays."

"My gun says he goes."

"You won't shoot me—at least not yet," Stefan said casually. "You must want something, and it would be utterly stupid to kill me and my friend Jason and have nothing to show for it."

She stood in silence and weighed her options. She did not put away the gun, but she did lower it. "Okay, at least make him sit in the corner. This is just between you and me."

"Jason, sit across from me. You don't belong in a corner," Stefan said. "You know all my secrets, so you might as well know this one. In fact, this is such a secret that I don't know what's going on inside her brain." He turned to her. "I don't know you, do I? To my knowledge I have never seen you before. But you come into my room with a gun and you start to make demands."

"I've come to talk to you about the diamonds."

"Is that a big surprise? Is it, Jason? I could have guessed that one myself." He looked at me and grinned, and then he turned toward her again. "Have you come to rob me? You think I have them in my suitcase or my closet perhaps?"

She stared at him. "I don't want the diamonds. I wouldn't know how to get rid of them. I only want money."

"How much money would you like me to give you?"

"Five million dollars. That really isn't much money for you. Give it to me and you'll never see me again.

And you'll never see my partner again either. I'll make sure of that."

"Who is your partner?"

A confused look passed over her face. "I thought you knew. Never mind who he is; I'll take care of him."

"You'll shoot him?"

"If necessary. Five million dollars can encourage me to do a lot of things."

"Who are you?"

"I suppose it's all right to tell you," she said. "Especially if we're going to be partners. My name is Janet Grand."

"And what do you know that would make it worth my giving you five million dollars?"

She said she had been in the car with the policeman when the courier was shot. "I know there was a mix-up and you ended up with diamonds and my friend ended up with paste."

"Hmm, is that how it is?"

She said she knew that Stefan had the jewelry or at least the proceeds from the sale of them. "Just give me five million dollars and you'll never see me or hear from me again."

"No."

"Think it through seriously. I can give you a day or two to get the money. That's not a large amount. I mean, it's not when you think how much you'll make off the deal, even if you have to discount them to someone."

"That's quite true. It's not a large amount, but I plan to return the stones."

"What? Are you insane? The insurance has already paid off—"

"I have had a change of heart."

"You haven't asked what I can give you for five million dollars."

"No, I haven't, but I assume this is more than a robbery."

"That's correct, and you know, of course, when you try to return the diamonds, they'll pin the courier's murder on you."

"Yes, I've thought about that. I had nothing to do with his death—"

"I know that fact and you know it, but you can't prove it. I can prove it."

"Really? How is that possible?"

"I was there when he was murdered." She told Stefan and me that she sat in the car. Until then she had not known anything about the theft. "But I was sort of dating that man. I don't even know his real name, but he liked me to call him Mastermind."

"Maybe he was trying to impress you."

"And he did. He wasn't a very nice man to be around most of the time, but he spent money on me and promised there would be a lot more in the future—a lot more." She shook her head. "But it never happened, and I have expensive tastes."

"So what do you know? What did you see?" Stefan asked.

"He shot the courier, and he grabbed what he thought were the real diamonds."

"Thank you for clearing this up, Janet."

"He'll kill you if you don't give me the money."

"Really? Is that something you know or something you hope?"

"He sent me today as his courier." She laughed. "Sounds like an important job, doesn't it?" She leaned closer to Stefan. "Let's keep it simple. You give me five million and—"

"I will give you nothing. Not a cent. Not a diamond."

"The Mastermind won't like this. He'll kill you and get everything."

Stefan stared. Never had I seen his eyes so hard and so determined. Finally he spoke quietly. "I am in God's hands."

She swore many angry words, but he said nothing more.

"You think God will protect you?"

"I am in His hands."

As if she had not heard, she asked, "Will God protect you if I shoot you?" She raised the gun.

"You won't kill me, because if you do, you won't find the diamonds. Neither will he."

"You think you're rather smart, don't you?"

Stefan stared at her and said slowly, "No, not really. If I had been smart, I wouldn't have gotten involved in such a nefarious deed. But as it is, I'm in God's hands."

"Will God protect you if he comes after you?"

"God will be with me because the Lord is with me now and won't forsake me or—"

"Whatever that means," she said. Vile words streamed from her mouth once again. "I suggest you rethink this visit. I can call you later tonight if—"

"No, don't bother. I won't change my mind."

"Maybe you'll think about it and decide to be sensible."

"No."

"I have one more proposition to offer you."

"I might as well hear it before I escort you from the room."

"I can give you a sworn statement about my partner, including the gun that fired the bullet that killed the courier. The gun still carries his fingerprints on it." She laughed. "But of course I'll have disappeared by the time you are ready to use the evidence."

"No."

"You don't want me to clear you of murder charges and keep you out of prison again?"

"My friend here, Jason Omore, once said something to me—something I've never forgotten."

"And I suppose I must listen to a sermon."

"Just this. At one point I wanted to do something morally questionable to achieve a moral objective—"

"What does that mean?"

"Forget the background. Jason's words were simple. He said we must never use the devil's tools to achieve God's work. He was right."

"Rather stupid reasoning—"

"No. This is the end of the discussion." Stefan stood up, took her arm, and led her toward the door. "I am not afraid. If you have a conscience, you'll turn over the evidence. If not, I won't buy my freedom from you. You or your Mastermind friend may kill me, but I will do the right thing."

"Don't be too sure—"

"You will never get the diamonds or the money. Never. I assure you of that."

Jason said, "That's how I remember it." He again wiped tears from his face.

"I'm sorry you had to relive that," I said. "Is there anything I can do?"

"No," he said and then added, "Wait. Come back in the morning. I do have something I should very much like you to do."

"What is that?" Ollie asked. "Did he give you the diamonds?"

"To me? Why should he have done that? Oh no."

"Okay, then tell us," Ollie said.

"Is not tomorrow satisfactory?"

"Tonight. Now. Right now is more satisfactory," Ollie said.

As he turned away from Ollie, Jason winked at me.

22

"Before I say more, I wish to have each of you wait for the morning light," Jason said. "My heart is very, very heavy over the loss of my friend, and it is most painful for me to speak."

"Why don't you take a short walk?" Burton suggested. "What you have to say may be important information." He nodded toward the detective and said, "He wants to clear this up as soon as possible."

"Yes, to be alone with my sorrow is a good idea, even for a brief time," Jason said. "I should like perhaps an hour."

Burton took Ollie's arm and mine, and we returned to the room. Once inside, Ollie picked up the phone and called the desk. He asked if we could have four sandwiches brought up. "Anything," he said and hung up. "So we wait."

I looked at Burton and tried to read his expression, but his face was inscrutable. He had learned something from that older couple, but he wasn't ready to tell me. And obviously he wasn't ready to tell the detective, who was his friend. I felt thoroughly confused.

Within fifteen minutes a waiter brought us sandwiches. Ollie started to dismiss him, but Burton handed the man a generous tip. All the sandwiches were chicken salad with fries on the side. The three of us ate while we waited for Jason.

Both men seemed to relax while they ate. Ollie lamented over a time when he and Burton had ordered hamburgers and fries at the Varsity—the original fast-food place—located near the Georgia Tech campus. It's supposed to have the longest counter in the world. I tried not to listen, but it was something about Ollie putting sugar in the saltshaker. He did it while Burton went to the restroom, and the other two students at the table eagerly waited for Burton to become the butt of the joke.

"But you got the best of us," Ollie said and turned to me. "Can you believe this part? That guy ate every single fry with all that sugar on them. At one point he sprinkled on even more sugar. The rest of us watched and were ready to laugh at him."

"I believe I also asked for a second serving—and ended up eating half of yours," Burton said.

"I've never figured out how anyone could put sugar on fries, not know the difference, and enjoy them."

"Oh, I didn't sprinkle sugar on the fries," Burton said.

"But I saw you. All three of us watched you!"

Burton shook his head. "I figured out what you did, Ollie. Sugar and salt are white, but they don't look exactly the same. Before I got to the table, I spotted the goofy expression on your faces. Just as I started to sit down, I watched Damon's eyes—he sat next to you—and he kept looking at the saltshaker. I caught on quickly. You didn't notice, but I grabbed a saltshaker from the table behind us and put the other in my pocket."

"Hey, he's smart." Ollie roared. "That's good! That's very good. All these years and I never knew."

"You always said I was smarter than you are," Burton said.

"But I didn't mean it," Ollie said. "Yet maybe you are. Maybe you are." He smiled, but something about his expression wasn't quite true.

Before I could figure out what was going on between them, Ollie launched into another story, but I stopped listening. I wanted to talk to Burton. Surely he had learned something from that couple in 624, and I felt increasingly anxious about it. I walked over to the window and looked out into the darkening evening as I tried to figure out how to get Burton alone.

Nothing came to mind. When I finally turned around, Ollie's back was to me, so I signaled Burton with my thumb, pointing to the door. He gave me the barest shake to indicate he didn't want to talk just then. I cocked my head and gave him my most quizzical expression.

Ollie must have noticed something and turned toward me.

Burton smiled at me and said to Ollie, "She grows on you, doesn't she?"

"Whatever," Ollie said. But what was supposed to sound indifferent carried a warm tone. He could be a nice man if he tried. And I wish he tried more often.

Exactly one hour later, Jason returned. To his credit, Ollie offered him the remaining sandwich. Jason took it and said, "To refuse a gift is to refuse a person. I shall eat it later, if I may. My heart does not desire food now."

Characteristically, Ollie said, "Okay, whatever works for you."

"You wish to know the rest of what I have to say," Jason said. The words came slowly at first, as if he had to force each one to the surface. "I shall tell you everything that I know."

The morning of the day that Stefan Lauber died, he and Jason met again for their regular study time together. Stefan asked questions about heaven—questions he had never asked before.

"I have not been there," Jason said and laughed, "so I can tell you only what appears in the Bible." For perhaps twenty minutes, he answered the things that troubled his friend. To most of the questions, he responded by turning to places in the Bible that provided answers.

"Of this you can be sure," Jason told him. "God will reward us by our deeds—by the things we have done after we have believed."

"And God does not hold our sins and failures against us—those we did before we believed?"

"God has promised us that it is like a marred sheet of paper that has been totally erased."

Jason said he felt those words brought comfort to Stefan.

"I believe that," Stefan said, "but I needed your assurance. I did many terrible things earlier in my life."

"But has not God forgotten them?" Jason said.

"But I still remember—"

"If you remember them, are you not doing a wrong thing? Why would you wish to remind God of things he has chosen to forget about your life?"

Instead of speaking, Stefan laughed before he hugged his friend.

After that they had prayer. When Jason got off his knees, Stefan said, "Wait. There is one thing." He handed Jason a large envelope. "My Bible is inside, and a letter."

"Why are you giving me your Bible?"

"I want you to have it," Stefan said. "I have another Bible here in my room, so I can read that one."

"This I do not understand."

Stefan put his hands on the young man's shoulders. "You have become the best friend I've ever had in my life. Ever. If something should happen to me—"

"Oh no, surely the woman did not mean—"

"She meant every word. Will her friend kill me? I don't know, but I will not change my mind. I must do what God wants me to do. I must return the diamonds."

"Where are they?"

As if he had not heard the question, Stefan said, "If something happens to me, inside this envelope is a letter. It tells my conversion story. At my funeral—"

"Oh, do not say such—"

"At my funeral, you must read the letter."

Jason began to protest, but Stefan hugged him. "Shh. This is not the time for protests from you. If I am still alive on Friday morning, you may return this envelope."

"Yes, I shall be most pleased to return this to you, but do not think of such thoughts—"

"If I am alive, you will return it."

Despite the continued protests, Stefan persisted and Jason agreed. "But I shall pray for our holy God to keep you alive."

"I would like to live, but I have made arrangements for myself and for all my funds to be used for the kingdom of God if I am not here."

Jason's voice cracked, and he couldn't talk anymore. I walked over to him and squeezed his hand. I had known Stefan only well enough that I had some sense of the African's loss.

"Where is the envelope?" Ollie asked. "Do you still have it?"

"Why would I not have it?"

"Would you get the envelope and bring it to us?" Ollie asked in a tightly controlled voice.

"It is for the funeral, is it not?"

"Bring it to me. Now. Here. To this room."

Jason looked at me and then at Burton as if to ask, "Should I?"

Both of us nodded.

"I shall do so," he said. "But one request: May I please hand it to you beside the lake? Outside I feel more—more at peace than I do in such a place as this."

"Whatever! Whatever! Just bring it."

As soon as he was gone from the room, Ollie said, "This is an interesting development, don't you think?"

"Yes," Burton said. "It's just as Julie said. We needed to ask the right questions."

The evening sky changed from crimson to ultramarine and finally to a dusky rose, and soon it would become a flat gray. In the metro area, the sky never becomes dark enough to see the fullness of the stars that look down at us. The three of us walked down toward the lake. The cicadas and the frogs seemed to compete in a cacophony of off-key notes. Despite that, the noise was soft enough not to distract.

We stopped by a small corner with chairs. A lamppost provided enough light to read.

Within minutes Jason found us. Without saying a word, he handed Ollie a large sealed envelope.

Ollie tore it open. He moved a few feet away to the lamppost where he could read and scanned the one-page letter. He could have read it where he stood, but I think he wanted to make certain none of us saw the contents.

I got up, walked over, and stood next to Ollie—more than anything just to show him we were in this together. Immediately I saw what the single sheet of paper was. "It's the same thing Lucas read," I said. "May we give it to him after the funeral? I'd like him to have a clean copy."

Ollie handed the single sheet to me and pulled out the Bible. It was large, mahogany colored with a cover made of skin.

"That is the skin of the zebra that covers the pages of the Holy Bible," Jason said. "Did I not give the Bible to him myself after his baptism?"

"A Bible," Ollie said. "This doesn't lead us anywhere." He almost tossed it aside, but he paused to flip idly through it as if he might find paper inserted between the pages. The Bible opened near the end, and at about the same time, both of us spotted a small key taped in the center between two columns.

"Ah, what is this?" Ollie untaped the key.

Jason walked over and watched Ollie carefully remove the key. "Do you not see where my friend placed it?" Jason said. He pointed to the underlined text: Romans 6:23.

"Guess that fits," Ollie said. He held the key to the light. He squinted to read the words. "It's the key to a safe-deposit box," he said. He turned it over and squinted again. He had to stare at it for several seconds before he said, "Bank of North Georgia."

"They have only half a dozen branches," I said. "So that shouldn't be a big task for the police."

"Where's the closest?" Ollie asked.

"Burton and I both live on the Southside, so I have no idea," I said.

"The bank? Surely it is the bank in Tucker," Jason said. "Would that not be correct? That is where I went with him on two occasions."

"Did you see what he did there?"

Jason shook his head. "But how could I? He went to a desk, held out his key, and the woman looked at it, checked his identification and signature, and took him into a room behind her."

"That's it," Ollie said. "I think we've found the missing diamonds." He thanked Jason and told him it was all right to leave. He handed the Bible to the African. "It's yours. Follow his wishes. His brother is in room 625. I assume he's already made plans for the funeral."

Jason left us, and the three of us headed back to the inn. We returned to the suite the Cartledge Inn had given us.

"One big problem has been solved," I said, "or so I assume. At least we think so. If the diamonds are there, that's one problem out of the way."

"But there have been two murders," Burton said. "That's more important than diamonds."

"Oh, we'll figure that out," Ollie said. "We won't close the door on this case."

"But some crimes never get solved, do they?" Burton said. He had a slight edge in his voice. Or did I only imagine it? I was glad he focused on the murders, because it was obvious Ollie had—at least for the moment—dismissed them from his thoughts.

"Why don't we call it a night?" Ollie said. "I'm absolutely worn out. I don't know why, but this has taken a lot out of me. You two might want to go for a proper dinner. I'm ready to turn in, and I live only ten minutes from here."

"Why don't you spend the night here?" Burton asked in a voice that was almost too casual.

"No trouble. It's a straight shoot off the Stone Mountain Expressway," Ollie said.

"I'd feel better if you stayed over," Burton said. "The desk can provide you with a toothbrush and razor."

I wasn't sure why that was significant, but I was ready to back Burton. "You know where the diamonds are, but no one else does," I said. "Jason does, too, but he was never a suspect. There has been just enough noise around here that someone—someone may still be searching."

"Two murders," Burton said. "We assume the same person killed them both. The three of us have been pretty visible all day."

"I'd like you to stay, Ollie." I turned on all the charm I could conjure and said softly, "Please."

"There are two king-sized beds," Burton said. "And one of those sofas folds into a bed. Julie could stay there."

"What? You think someone's going to shoot one of you?"

"Or shoot you maybe," I said. "Two murders. Who knows what else may happen?"

Ollie seemed to think about it for a few seconds. "Sure, why not? If you two will feel safer—"

"I'll feel much safer being with you," Burton said and laughed.

"Now I'm the hero?" Ollie laughed, too. "Yeah, okay, let's do it."

Ollie decided he did want to eat after all, so all three of us went to the dining room. On the way we stopped at the desk and asked them to make up the sofa for me.

"Immediately," Craig said.

When we stood at the entrance of the dining room, I was impressed by the soft decor with its muted tones and earth-colored table linen. The area featured two sections—the casual room and the formal room. The maître d' suggested we choose the room on our right. "Do not be concerned about your dress. This is not about clothing," he said with a slight European accent. "This is about cuisine. To your left is strictly American." He wasn't able to disguise his disdain before he smiled and said, "But in this direction is the finest European cuisine. We have three chefs, all trained in Europe and—"

"You sold me, pal," Ollie said. "Let's go continental."

A uniformed waiter came immediately and filled our water glasses and offered delicate pieces of mint, lime, or orange. At my urging, we all took mint.

Ollie didn't seem to care what he ordered, so the waiter, whose name tag identified him as Henri, suggested chicken in aspic, asparagus, coeur de crème, and wild strawberries for dessert. After Ollie nodded, the waiter said in a heavy accent, "That is an excellent choice."

I settled for a Caesar salad and yellowfin tuna on pasta and no dessert. I didn't get the enthusiasm for my choice, but the waiter did say, "Our tuna is imported, as you may assume, from Australia. It was brought in fresh this morning. You are most discerning, madam."

Burton chose the veal cutlet and the wild strawberries.

"The veal. . .ahh, my dear sir, that is my absolute favorite," the waiter said. "The veal is paper-thin and encrusted in a delicate mixture of spices, egg, and bread crumbs. It is the most delicious thing we offer this evening."

We didn't talk much during the dinner, except about the food. We all agreed that it was absolutely delicious.

"At these prices, it needs to be," Ollie said.

"The meal is on me," Burton said. "Please. I can get mine free, but I'd like to pay for all three."

I smiled at Burton and said softly, "Oh, is this like a date?"

Burton blushed.

I loved that response.

23

O n the way back to the room, Ollie picked up a fairly expensive "Male Pak" from the desk. The female clerk made me a "Female Pak," as well. "There is no charge for this." Her long brown hair covered up her name tag, but I assumed she must be Doris. It was the first time I hadn't seen Craig behind the desk.

When I asked about the sofa, she smiled and said, "The housekeeper has taken care of it."

We went inside the room and found that all three beds had been made and pulled back. On each bed was a small bar of Zhocolate. To my surprise, Ollie knew it. "Hey, this is supposed to be the best chocolate in the world—and probably the most expensive."

We each munched our Zhocolate and agreed it was rich and that a two-ounce bar was enough. Ollie started in on one of his stories about getting some college girl to bake chocolate pies.

"Hey, guys, how about if you go into your room and tell your stories? I'll use the bathroom while you guys relive the glory days." I didn't give them an opportunity to argue.

"I'll run out to the car and get my stuff," Burton said.

Inside the bathroom I saw two white terry bathrobes hanging up, and I claimed one of them.

"In case you're worried," Burton said, standing in the doorway of his room, "we'll lock the door. It has a lock on the inside. It makes a loud racket—in case—"

I started to make a smart remark, but instead I said, "With two strong men behind a lock in the next room, I know I'll be safe."

"Oh, and we have our own bathroom, so we won't disturb you in any way." He turned to close the door.

"Uh, about that—that visit you made to—"

"Later. Trust me." Burton closed the door. I heard the lock turn.

Despite the closed door, after I went to bed, I could still hear Ollie's voice. I didn't have to listen to his stories, but every few minutes I heard his loud guffaw.

With such discordant music in my ears, I finally drifted off to sleep. I didn't sleep well because I kept thinking of poor Stefan and Deedra Knight. I wondered if the police would ever find out who murdered them. As I lay in the dark, I tried to imagine every possible thing that could have transpired between Burton and the couple in 624. Despite his closed lips, I sensed it was important information.

By seven both men moved around inside their locked room, and they didn't do it on tiptoes. At exactly 7:45 a waiter brought us breakfast. Apparently Ollie had ordered from room service instead of our going down for it. When they came out of the room fully dressed, Ollie pointed to an ugly greenish-and-yellow omelet. I spotted cold cereal and opted for that, and so did Burton. All three of us poured from the two carafes of coffee.

"The bank opens at nine," Burton said. As he put down his third cup of coffee, he checked his watch. "That gives us forty-five minutes. I'll be glad to drive."

"Thanks, chum, but no." Ollie shook his head.

"No, this is strictly police business. I'll take care of it, but I'll call you."

"I'd like to go with you," Burton said in a strong voice.

"That's not necessary." He smiled before he said, "You two are civilians. I allowed you to sit through all of this out of professional courtesy and—"

"I really want to go with you," Burton said. He smiled and added, "In fact, I insist."

Just then a conversation from the day before snapped into my head. I understood why Burton persisted. "Yes, and I'd like to be along as well," I said.

"I appreciate your help," Ollie said. He smiled at me this time. "Both of you. Because of you, I hope this is just about over."

"But it's not over," Burton said. "The diamonds won't be found."

Ollie looked dazed as if Burton had slugged him. "But I have the key—"

"No, they won't be found," I said, "because you'll have them."

"What are you—are you trying to say that I'd steal them?"

I stared at Burton. "Your old classmate catches on faster than I thought."

"Hey, where do you get off talking to me like—?"

"Okay, then prove it," I said. "Call your supervisor or whatever you call the person above you and explain about the key you found inside the Bible."

"Sounds like a good idea," Burton said.

"You're serious. You think I would rip off the diamonds," Ollie said. "You two aren't joking, are you?"

"Unless murder is a joke," Burton said. "No, we're not joking. Maybe we can't get you convicted for the murder of Jeremiah Macgregor—"

"Or Stefan Lauber or Deedra Knight," I added, interrupting Burton.

"But we can stop you from stealing the diamonds—the real ones this time."

"This is too insulting to discuss." Ollie pushed past me and started toward the door.

"Okay, Mastermind," Burton said. "Stop."

Ollie turned around and stared at both of us. "You don't seriously—"

"That's what you called yourself in college. You remember, Ollie, when you did all those pranks and underhanded tricks."

"That's what I remembered," I said. "Mastermind. You used the word yourself, Ollie."

"This is nuts," he said and walked past Burton.

Burton grabbed him from behind and held him in a headlock. "And before you tell me I'm assaulting an officer of the court or whatever you're supposed to tell me, I admit my guilt. Either give me the key or use your cell to call your supervisor."

"I will not give in to your tactics." Ollie could barely speak. "Ease up—let me breathe."

Just as Burton relaxed his grip slightly, Ollie punched him with his left arm, broke the hold, and in record time pulled out his gun with the other hand. "Now back off. You are interfering with an investigation, and you are obstructing justice."

"If we let you go, we obstruct justice," Burton said.

"You'll have to kill both of us," I said. I almost

laughed at those words. I'd heard them so many times on TV.

"What are two more dead bodies?" he asked. His gaze shifted from me to Burton and back again. "I don't want to hurt either of you, but if you force me, I'll shoot you right now."

This wasn't funny, and it wasn't TV. That's when the criminal is supposed to crack or give up or do something stupid. Ollie had a gun, and we had nothing. He only needed two bullets and a second between shots.

"You will have to kill me," Burton said, "because I won't let you out of this room with that key."

Ollie raised the gun. "This is my last warning."

A knock at the door interrupted us. I was less than three feet from the door, so I lurched forward and opened it.

Ollie fired.

24

I pulled the door open at the moment of the shot.

Jason stood outside the door and stared at us. "I came because—because—"

I turned around. Burton had grabbed Ollie, and they grappled for the gun. Blood seeped from Burton's right shoulder, but he still fought. I raced over to the scuffle. I had received all kinds of training in self-defense, but none of it seemed appropriate. I did the most natural thing that came to me: I grabbed Ollie's left hand. I bit the soft spot between his thumb and index finger. And I bit down hard.

Ollie tried to shrug me away. Just that motion was all it took for Burton to use both of his hands to pound Ollie's right wrist against the floor. The crack of the bone filled the room. Ollie no longer resisted.

"Now it's over," Burton said.

I pulled out my cell and dialed 911.

Jason stepped into the room. "I came to this door because of bad feelings in my heart. I cannot explain except that I did not feel it was good for that man to have the key."

"You saved our lives," I said.

"Yes, this must be so," Jason said. "And even more so is that God helped me to do just that." He winked. "Is that not so?"

———

Burton's gunshot wound bled quite a bit, but it was

BANDAGE

superficial: He needed only a large ~~bondage~~ from the hotel's first-aid kit.

After the police arrived, Burton told them his conversation with the couple in 624. At last I was able to find out.

After I'd knocked on the door and the old man answered and his wife behind him, they had accused me of being the bad cop in the TVish good cop/bad cop scenario and wouldn't talk to me, so I left.

"They didn't want to talk to me either," Burton said, "but I think they were afraid not to. This is what happened," he started.

"Are you from the police?" the old man asked. "From the same place as the other one?"

Before I could answer, the woman said, "No, this one isn't cruel like that one." She walked up to me and peered into my face. "You're not going to threaten us, are you?"

"No, ma'am, I wouldn't threaten you. I don't do things like that."

"That's good. One death threat is enough."

They had already acted odd, and I wasn't sure what to make of that statement, so I decided to try humor. "Why, you're both too nice for anyone to hurt."

"What kind of cop are you anyway?" the woman said.

"I'm not a policeman. I didn't mean to mislead you—"

"Then why are you here? Why do you want to

know about 623?" her husband asked.

"It's like this: I'm a pastor. The woman who came to the room with me is a psychologist. We're both guests at the hotel. Julie doesn't have a room, but she is a guest. The lead homicide detective is a close friend. He asked us to help him with this case."

"Mama, it's just like *Murder She Wrote*. Remember that? That Jessica Fletcher wasn't with the police, but she solved most of the crimes for them. And she did tricks like that—let people think she was someone she wasn't. You must be a pretty smart fella."

The woman came up close again and stared into my eyes. She nodded twice before she grabbed both my hands. Her fingers lightly traced my palms and the back of my hands, even though her gaze stayed on my face. "You have good hands. They feel honest." She turned to her husband. "Papa, I think we can trust him."

"I appreciate—"

"You have good hands," the woman said again. "I was a manicurist for forty-three years. When I see hands, I know the person. They say eyes don't lie, but I can tell you that hands don't lie. Yes, you are a good man."

"Thank you—"

"You need a little work on your nails, but your hands are good. I learn much from observing hands."

"So you'll tell me what I want to know?"

"Of course," he said. He pulled up three chairs in a kind of triangular shape. She raised her hand as if to say, "Just wait." Without asking me, she hurried into the bathroom and minutes later came out with a pot of tea. While she was gone, he told me his name was

Duncan Kyle and she was his wife of forty-five years and her name was Mildred.

"Not Millie," she called out. "Just Mildred. Now you must join us," she said and poured each of us a cup. They had their cups drained before I had taken more than a few sips. I don't know much about tea, but my nose told me she had blended in several different herbs.

I took a sip and wished I hadn't. I'm not much of a tea drinker anyway, but to be polite, I took another sip while they watched.

I was afraid they were going to ask about the tea, so I said, "Look, can you help us? We think you know something about the murder across the hall."

"What are you talking about?" the man asked. "We know nothing."

"After the murder, you both went to the gazebo and discussed the matter. Someone heard you talking."

"Just like that Jessica Fletcher, isn't he?" the woman said. She shook her head, but it was obvious she was impressed. She turned to her husband. "Tell him, Papa."

"It wasn't much. We heard a noise. I'm not even sure what it was, but it was like a loud pop."

"No, Papa, more like a car backfiring. That's how Jessica's witnesses always describe it. And that is exactly how it sounded to us."

"Okay, maybe so," he said. "Yes, I did think maybe it was a gunshot. I used to do some target practice. I haven't done any for maybe twenty years, but people like me never forget the sound."

"So what did you do?"

"Nothing," the man said. "I mean, we talked about it, but that was about all—"

"And what time was that?"

"A few minutes after six. Five after at most," she said. "Remember—we had just heard the top-of-the-hour headline news on CNN."

"Right, yes," he said. "We had eaten a big lunch and didn't want dinner, but we decided to go for a walk."

As they left the room, he turned around to lock the door. Just then the door to room 623 opened.

"That man was startled, I tell you," she said. "He still had a gun in his hand."

"How long after the shot was that?"

They looked at each other and couldn't decide if it had been ten minutes or fifteen. They decided no more than fifteen, but probably a little less. That would have made it around 6:20. That still would have given Lucas time to come into the room before the food gurney.

"I don't think he was aware he still had the gun in his hand," she said. "Not until he saw my face."

"Then I was the stupid one. I turned to Mama and said, 'See, I told you it was gunfire. I knew it!' Just as I said those words, I knew I was in trouble."

"The man walked right up to us and put the gun to Mama's head. I'd seen it done on TV, but this was real and it was a gun. He said, 'I just killed one man. I can kill you two.' "

"'Please,' Mama whimpered," Duncan said. "I was scared, and my Mildred, she was even more scared."

She started to deny it and then said, "Yes, I was plenty scared."

"If you forget you saw me," the man said, "I'll forget I saw you. If you should remember, I'll come after you. I can get your name at the desk, and I'll come and shoot both of you and burn down your house."

"I didn't see anything," Duncan told him.

"I told the man the same thing," Mildred said.

"He told us to go back inside and count to fifty before we came back out, and that's exactly what we did. He said if we should see him again, he would be a total stranger."

"Did you see him again?" I asked.

They stared at each other. Duncan nodded.

"He was with the other police," Mildred said. "Except they were in uniforms. He wasn't. He wore a suit."

"He stared at us, and when no one else was looking our way, he drew his index finger across his throat."

By then I had it figured out, but I needed to have them tell me. "What did he look like?"

"Big, oh, he was so tall," the man said. Duncan was barely over five feet, so I assumed even I looked tall to him.

"His hair was not blond, but it was not dark," she said.

"Eyes?" I asked. "Did you notice his eyes?"

"Green with tiny specks of brown," she said. "Very tiny specks."

The eyes. I had looked into them too many times in the past not to recognize them. Sadness filled my heart. I knew Ollie was capable, but it was still a shock. I asked if there was anything else they could tell me.

"After they came—the police—we went into the parking lot and discussed this," Mildred said. "We have not been out of the room since then."

"Will you catch him?" the old man asked. "Have

you collected the vital clues to solve this?"

"Not quite," I said. "There is something else I have to learn first, but I'm very close."

I don't know why but I asked, "What about this man? The man with the gun? Is there anything else you can tell me?"

"He's on drugs," Mildred said. "Perhaps not the first time with the gun, but when he returned. Definitely on drugs."

"I doubt—"

"For forty-three years I was in the business. During the last ten years, I fired many women who could not leave the drugs alone. I know what I know. He was on drugs."

"You're sure?" I could hardly believe that.

"Listen to Mama. She may not always be right, but when it comes to the hands, she is never wrong. Tremors. Look at the tremors. Then you know."

Burton shook his head and stared at me. "As she said those words, I realized that I had observed the tremors. I'd been so preoccupied with other things, that fact hadn't registered."

25

There isn't much left to tell, and this isn't an old TV script in which the hero explains everything. We had no trouble implicating Ollie. We also learned that he had come to the Cartledge Inn after he had called in sick.

It was also common knowledge at DeKalb headquarters that he and Deedra Knight had once been involved. She and Ollie hadn't been together for a couple of years. I suppose it was a case of thieves falling out with each other.

As for Pam Harty, we learned she had once been Ollie's housemate—the term used by one of his neighbors. After she was arrested, Pam didn't want to testify against Ollie. She loved him, and as she said, "I don't want to be the cause of his going to prison." At first she insisted she was afraid to speak up and that he had threatened her.

After she received a promise of immunity, was assured that Ollie wouldn't hurt her, and (even more important) was told that she was only one of his many girlfriends, she told us everything. She produced concrete evidence to convict Oliver Viktor. As they say in the old gangster films, "That canary sure could sing." She told a lot about Ollie—much more than we had expected.

When the police raided his house, they found evidence of other crimes. I also learned that he hadn't lied to me about his so-called motor-system disorder.

He had a disorder, all right, but it was because he was addicted to a drug called oxycodone. It's an opiate and highly addictive. It created symptoms similar to those of Parkinson's disease, but it was caused by a lengthy use of oxycodone. That explained a lot of things about his behavior.

⸺

When Burton and I were finally free late that night from all the official police questions of Ollie's arrest, I was utterly worn out. And so was Burton. He went to his room, and I decided to book a room. Craig was on duty, and when I told him I wanted a room, I added, "Anything but 623."

"That's still not open anyway," he said, "so I can't let you have it."

He hadn't caught my humor, and I didn't argue with him. I was mentally wiped out. I went to the room, number 509, and fell across the bed, and I don't remember anything until the phone rang.

"Hey, this is that guy who slept in the next room last night. I liked your snoring so much, I want to take you to dinner."

"I don't snore."

"You don't know for sure, though, do you?" Burton said. "Hey, it's almost 8:00. Can you wash your face and be ready in thirty minutes?"

"How about ten minutes?"

Exactly eight minutes later he was waiting by the elevator.

He hugged me.

"That wasn't the kind of hug you give a parishioner," I said. "I know the difference."

"I'm glad you know the difference." That smile again followed his words. If we hadn't been in public, I would have kissed him.

"I don't know what happened to you," he said, "but I know it happened. You believe, don't you?"

As we walked toward the dining room, I said, "It is so weird. I do believe. I can't explain why or how or—"

"That's why we call it faith," he said. "It isn't anything we can tear apart and examine. Either we believe or we don't."

Instead of going into the dining room, Burton took my arm and propelled me right out the front door. We walked toward the car park and were perhaps a hundred feet from the main entrance.

"That's far enough," he said. He pulled me into a dark alcove and embraced me. "I love you, Julie West. You're crazy, and you drive me nuts, and there are times I'd like to put a muzzle on your smart mouth, but I can't think of any other woman in the world I'd rather fall in love with than you."

"I should hope you wouldn't." I kissed him, and then I said, "This is so special to me. When I came here yesterday, I was trying to figure out how to get you out of my heart."

"And I came to the Cartledge Inn to ask God's help to get you out of my life."

"I'll bet God is smiling at us right now."

"I don't know," he said, "but I'll bet He likes to see *us* smile."

Burton wouldn't let me answer. He kissed me again.

"I still have questions. Millions of them."

He put out his hand and touched mine.

In the alcove, we were two shadows that faced each other. The darkness blotted out our expressions and momentarily erased my questions.

In his secret past, **Cecil Murphey** has written eleven romantic-suspense novels with female pseudonyms (and it's a secret because he won't divulge his aliases). Although not always credited, he has written or cowritten more than one hundred books, including the New York Times's bestseller *90 Minutes in Heaven*. He cowrote *Gifted Hands: The Ben Carson Story*, which has been continuously in print since 1990. Under his own name, he has written such nonfiction books as *When Someone You Love Suffers from Depression or Mental Illness*. Cecil and his wife, Shirley, live near Stone Mountain, Georgia, where the novel takes place. In his next novel, *Everybody Called Her a Saint*, he has decided to kill someone in Antarctica (where he has traveled). Please visit his Web site at www.cecilmurphey.com.

You many correspond with this author by writing:
Cecil Murphey
Author Relations
PO Box 721
Uhrichsville, OH 44683

A Letter to Our Readers

Dear Reader:
In order to help us satisfy your quest for more great mystery stories, we would appreciate it if you would take a few minutes to respond to the following questions. We welcome your comments and read each form and letter we receive. When completed, please return to:

Fiction Editor
Heartsong Presents—MYSTERIES!
PO Box 721
Uhrichsville, Ohio 44683

Did you enjoy reading *Everybody Wanted Room 623* by Cecil Murphey?

Very much! I would like to see more books like this! The one thing I particularly enjoyed about this story was:

_____
_____
_____

Moderately. I would have enjoyed it more if:

_____
_____
_____

Are you a member of the HP—MYSTERIES! Book Club?
Yes   No

If no, where did you purchase this book?

_____

Please rate the following elements using a scale of 1 (poor) to 10 (superior):

___ Main character/sleuth   ___ Romance elements

___ Inspirational theme   ___ Secondary characters

___ Setting   ___ Mystery plot

How would you rate the cover design on a scale of 1 (poor) to 5 (superior)? _____

What themes/settings would you like to see in future **Heartsong Presents—MYSTERIES!** selections? _____

_____

_____

_____

Please check your age range:
- Under 18
- 18–24
- 25–34
- 35–45
- 46–55
- Over 55

Name: _____

Occupation: _____

Address: _____

E-mail address: _____

OHIO
Weddings

3 stories in 1

Secrets, love, and danger are afoot when three remarkable women reexamine their lives on Bay Island. Lauren Wright returns to straighten out her past only to disrupt her future. Becky Merrill steps onto the shore and into sabotage. Judi Rydell can't outrun her former life. Who will rescue their hearts?

ISBN 978-1-59789-987-1
Contemporary, paperback, 352 pages

Please send me _____ copies of *Ohio Weddings*. I am enclosing $7.97 for each.
(Please add $3.00 to cover postage and handling per order. OH add 7% tax.
If outside the U.S. please call 740-922-7280 for shipping charges.)

Name_____

Address _____

City, State, Zip _____

To place a credit card order, call 1-740-922-7280.
Send to: Heartsong Presents Readers' Service, PO Box 721, Uhrichsville, OH 44683